T0265211

18 17 16 15 1 2 3 4



*Published by* Blue Dome Press
335 Clifton Avenue, Clifton
New Jersey 07011, USA

www.bluedomepress.com

Library of Congress Cataloging-in-Publication Data Available

*Translated by* Aslı Sancar

ISBN: 978-1-935295-85-3

*Printed by*
Imak Ofset, Istanbul - Turkey

# THE SERVANT

Cenk Enes Özer

NEW JERSEY • LONDON • FRANKFURT • CAIRO

# My Heedlessness, My Captivity

*"Don't be one of those who die in their twenties and are buried in their eighties!"*

It was an ordinary day when the sun rose from the same side, the leaves fell towards the ground, and the clouds made people shiver. Again the civil servants who would have their breakfast in the office filled the shuttle buses, the students who would finish their homework at recess waited for the school buses, and again the sounds of the shops' metal shutters were firing at each other. There was nothing to distinguish this day from other days. Or there was no one who noticed the difference.

Yağmur[1] was one of the lucky ones who were able to have breakfast at home. However, he still had not been able to escape from the effects of the dream he saw, for he was not at all hungry. Several sips of tea and three or four olives—the seeds of which he swallowed with difficulty—were enough. In order not to be late, he immediately got

---

[1] In Turkish, *yağmur* (pronounced [ˈjaːmur]) means "rain." (All footnotes are those of the editor.)

up, put on his shoes and left. As always, he took the key chain from the right-front section of his bag, found the right key without even looking, and again locked the door twice. When the elevator he called came to his floor, he got on and pressed the ground floor button which had already been pressed. At that moment he remembered again the dream that had made him uneasy, in fact, had startled him. The details were not very clear in his mind; however, the shouts of the person who had introduced himself as "Servant" were still ringing in his ears: "Aren't you tired of this monotony?"

Apparently someone had pushed the "call" button on the elevator from the ground floor. It was obvious that the elevator was going to the ground floor. Then what made him feel he must push that button any way? What was really strange was that when he reached the ground floor and opened the door, he didn't see anyone. His uneasiness turning into anxiety reminded Yağmur of the horror film he had watched before he went to sleep. He dismissed his feelings by saying to himself, "All of this must be from the influence of the film I watched."

While walking towards the garage, Yağmur took the car keys from the left-hand compartment of his briefcase. Without looking, he extended his hand and pressed the remote control button to open the car door. Although he saw that the door locks did not open, he couldn't help but pull on the handle of the door. Of course, it did not open. Pushing the remote control button a little harder, he again pulled on the handle of the door with his other hand.

Obviously the remote control battery was dead. But that was not what made him mad; what angered Yağmur was his doing the same thing he had done on the elevator. Pulling on the door although the lock had not opened was actually a stupid and unnecessary thing. Just like pressing on the ground floor button that was lit up. Plus, wasn't there that strange voice echoing in his ear: "Aren't you tired of this monotony?"

Opening the car door with the key, Yağmur got into his car and just sat there for some time. He couldn't help but think, "I get up at the same time every morning and get ready to go to work. I go on the same road to the office and always do the same job. I take a lunch break at the same time every day and leave work at the same time every evening. I go home on the same road and eat dinner as my first task. Then I sit in front of the television and watch the same TV series, magazine programs and movies every evening. After that I go to bed at the same time and always toss and turn for the first half hour. Every day resembles the previous day so much that if someone would ask, "What day is it?" it's not possible for me to give a correct answer the first time. Of course, except for paydays. By the way, isn't today payday?"

After setting out and going about twenty meters, Yağmur stopped behind the cars lined up in the heavy traffic. This was a rare situation for the avenue just in front of his house. If you looked at the people running on the sidewalk, it was clear that something had happened. But in spite of this commotion going on around him, Yağmur was focused on something else. A new building had been built on the empty lot located close to his apartment building. It was not a building under construction; it was basically finished with curtains at the windows and clothespins on the balcony. He was astonished. "How is this possible? I have been living here for approximately five years. I use this avenue every morning and evening. I remember well that there was an empty lot here when we moved in, because whenever we gave directions to our house, we said, "The second building next to the empty lot on the street." He quickly got out of his car. Passing through the people who were running towards the place of the event, Yağmur approached one of the shops beneath the new apartment building. The shop owner was standing at the door looking anxiously toward the crowd and trying to understand what had happened.

"Excuse me, how long have you been here?" Yağmur asked curiously.

But the answer of the shop owner could not quench this curiosity:

"About ten minutes. According to what I heard, a man had a heart attack at the steering wheel. Then he hit the pole in the middle of the road. May God have mercy on his soul."

"No, I didn't mean that. This shop, this building—I am curious as to how long they have been here."

"It's been a month since I opened this shop, but the building was finished about four months ago."

Without even saying, "Have a good day," to his old new neighbor, Yağmur left. In spite of the crowd that had formed thirty meters away, he stood in front of the six-storey building that he had just become aware of and, raising his head, he took a long look at the building that had not been built overnight. Then his eyes turned to the uneasy agitated crowd. He thought about the man who had died from a heart attack. Yağmur said to himself, "Maybe he had never seen this building like me." While thinking, "If death is breaking off from what is happening in life, then what is the difference between us," these words he had heard somewhere came to his mind:

"Don't be one of those who die in their twenties and who are buried in their eighties!"

Now he understood better these words that he had heard a long time ago.

Yağmur suddenly became startled by a honking horn. As the traffic slowly began to move, he ran quickly towards his car which was in the middle of the road; he got behind the wheel and began to move. As he passed by the car that had hit the pole, it never occurred to him that he would see the car of his dreams like this...

# Those Who Find Are Seekers

"*Everyone who seeks cannot find, but those who find are seekers.*" Bayazid Bistami.[2]

Yağmur entered the office upset for being late. Today was payday and as an accounting manager, there was a lot of work to be done.

He said good morning to everyone and sat down at his desk. While looking at the list of things to be done, he said, "Selma, by 10:30 have the salaries pre.." But raising his head, he saw that Selma was not there.

Although he asked where Selma was, no one said anything. At that moment Selma came into the room carrying a birthday cake with burning candles on top. While putting aside the papers in her other hand, everyone began to sing in unison: "Happy birthday, Yağmur!" He wasn't even aware that today was his birthday. Just like he wasn't aware of the building on the empty lot or that Selma wasn't even in the room. After a few minutes of

---

2 Abu Yazid (Bayazid) Bastami (804–874), one of the greatest Sufi masters.

celebration, Selma brought the papers she had put on her desk a few minutes ago.

"Sir, these are the company invoices, but I don't know what this is." Yağmur put the invoices aside and opened a blank, sealed envelope. There was a note inside:

> "*I congratulate you not because you came into this world years ago, but because you will be born today. If you are tired of the monotony, find me. But don't forget! Everyone who seeks cannot find, but those who find are seekers.*" Servant...

He was just forgetting about all the strange things that had happened since morning, when this message shocked him like a cold shower. Looking around, he tried to disguise his amazement. Everyone was busy with his work.

Who was this "Servant"? Where and how should I look for him? Plus, why should I look for him?

Everyone was looking at him, and Tayfun asked, "Did you say something to me, sir?" Maybe he was thinking out loud due to his astonishment. He felt embarrassed and was only able to say "No."

Yağmur made it through the day with difficulty. In addition to the pressure of paying salaries, the whole day passed with the question, "Who is Servant?" This was such a thought that it contained both a sweet curiosity and a foreboding fear. The fear of the unknown was mixed with the desire to know it, and it was turning into an indescribable feeling that he had never felt before. Either he would escape from him or search for him. Actually Yağmur didn't want to do either, but the feeling of urgency inside him was dragging him towards a point of decision. And with full speed...

"The note said, 'If you are tired of the monotony, find me.' Wasn't it the monotony that was the cause of my weariness? Today is my birthday and I have served a full thirty-two years in this world prison. At times I described for minutes dreams that I had seen for seconds. But now if someone said, 'Tell me about the thirty-two years,' there was so little to tell. Every day was the same; what could I tell? Even if I lived another thirty-two years, it was obvious that I wouldn't have much to tell about. When I was small my grandfather would say, 'They will ask how you spent your life, my sweetheart.' What will I say to those who ask? Will I say, 'I don't have anything to say. You know, the same...' No, no... I am really upset. For God's sake, what do I have to lose? OK, but how will I find this Servant? Moreover, he wrote something like 'Those who seek cannot find; those who find do not seek...' Now I'm really confused." Saying this, Yağmur began laughing to himself, probably because his nerves were on edge.

He thought of similar situations in some films he had watched. There must be a clue in the note. On his way home, he began to think about the other sentence in the note: "I congratulate you not because you came into this world years ago, but because you will be born today." He wrote as if "coming into this world" and "being born" were different things. According to him, coming to this world was nothing to celebrate. What should be celebrated is "being born." We say that babies who leave their mother's womb and begin to live in this world have been "born." This means that being born means beginning to live. Then I am going to be born today; in other words, I am going to begin living. Strange. Wasn't I living until today? Was I dead? Wait a minute... Wasn't I? What was my difference from the man who had a heart attack this morning? He didn't see the building on the empty lot and neither did I. When I entered the office and greeted everyone, Selma was not there, but I didn't realize it. The dead do not hear, see or know those around them. What is my difference? Just as I am unaware during my sleep... At any rate, don't they call sleep a small death? So it can be understood that we pass our time other than sleep in sleepwalking. In other words, we are sleeping all day. Or all our lives...

He arrived home with these thoughts in his mind. While entering the garage, he looked at the new building out of the corner of his eye. The things he had lived throughout the day passed quickly before his eyes. It had been a long and tiring day. But he didn't feel at all tired like he felt on the previous days. When he entered the house, he smelled his favorite food. Apparently his wife had not forgotten that today was his birthday. When she heard the sound of the door, she appeared from the kitchen and said:

"Happy birthday!"

Yağmur replied, "I don't know about the day I came to this world, but today is truly my birthday." His wife looked startled. He added, "I'm coming as soon as I wash my hands." Throughout dinner he talked about the events of the day.

Yağmur had so much to talk about that Rehnüma didn't have a chance to speak.

Finally she asked, "How are you going to find this Servant?" This question was enough to suddenly send Yağmur, who had been speaking non-stop for almost an hour, into silence and, in fact, a little hopelessness. Fortunately Rehnüma had an idea so this anxiety-laden situation didn't last too long:

"My father would always say, 'Everyone who seeks cannot find, but those who find are seekers.' One day I curiously asked him what this meant. He said, 'Seek! Seek without getting fed up or tired! Prove you yearn for what you love with your effort! At that moment a hand will touch your shoulder, and what you have been seeking will find you...'"

"Absolutely," Yağmur said after thinking about it a little. "Maybe I won't be able to find what I am looking for, but it will find me! Just like in my dream last night..."

Now he was impatient to go to bed. Now his bed was no longer a coffin in his eyes, but a mother's womb from which he was going to be reborn. First he made ablution and then, sitting up in bed, he quickly recited all the prayers he knew. Then he opened his hands and tried to express what was coming from his inner world:

"My God! Just as I have not lived until today, You count it like that too. Accept my birth as getting up from bed this morning. See and show my awakening from sleep as my escape from heedlessness. Just as the morning sun drives out the darkness, the evening breeze disperses the clouds, and the nighttime moon illuminates our world, You drive out the darkness of sin from my heart and illuminate the world of my heart. Amen!"

While these words were falling from his tongue, even he was surprised by such a heart-felt flow of words. Like when a person speaks a language in his dream that he doesn't know; this was something like that. It was as if he was not speaking, but was being made to speak. Now, without enduring any more thought, his poor mind fell asleep...

# Strange Encounter

He got up in the morning... Yes, that's all. There was nothing else to say about the whole night. He slept and he woke up. That's all! In a strange way he felt the pain in his heart of having been deceived. Without thinking about any details, he externalized his anger: "No, the stupidity is with me! The man said, 'If you seek, you won't find.' What more should he say?"

When he washed his face, he came to himself a little. Now he could think more clearly. Why had he become angry? The Servant hadn't given his word. He wasn't saying, "You keep looking; I will find you anyway." The best thing to do in the situation was to "actively" wait. And actually this was not going to continue for long...

Now he was trying to see every thing he looked at with his eyes and to hear every sound with his ears. In other words, he was seeking. There might be a clue to find him in his surroundings. At that moment a sound from outside caught his attention. He went to the living room which faced the street and opened the window. The sound resembled a *sala*.[3] He realized that he had heard this sound many

---

[3] A call to a funeral service.

times until now, but that he had never listened to it. This time he listened very carefully for he was seeking:

"Yağmur, son of Osman from the district of Mucur in Kırşehir, died last night. His funeral will be held today after the Noon Prayer and the body will be buried in the Metropolitan Municipality's Graveyard for the Destitute. May God have mercy on him!"

Just as when although a person knows he has not done anything, when he sees the persistent claims of those around him, he begins to doubt himself and almost believes the others, this was the exact same situation. He collapsed in his shoes. He thought about finding the mosque where the *sala* was coming from to learn about what was happening, but he couldn't move. In fact, when he realized that he was not able to inhale, he wanted to shout at the top of his lungs. He wanted to hold onto life; it was as if he was being forcefully taken to the Graveyard for the Destitute in a coffin. His wife Rehnüma hurriedly entered the living room. When Yağmur had fallen to the floor, the vase on top of the cover he had pulled down made such a crash that everyone except Yağmur had heard it. Rehnüma put her arms around her husband and tried to get him up from the floor. On the one hand, she became really concerned when she saw his lusterless eyes and, on the other hand, she was trying to suppress her helplessness with screams. Coming to himself at that moment, Yağmur hugged his wife and tried to calm her down:

"Stop! Stop! Don't get upset! It's OK; there's nothing wrong. Calm down! My head just spun around for a moment; that's all. I guess my blood pressure fell."

He quickly got ready so as not to be late for work. For he had to stop by the mosque as soon as possible to see what was going on. But then it occurred to him that the *hodja*[4] who called the *sala* would not be there. The only remaining way to face the truth was for him to attend his own Funeral Prayer. This idea seemed very strange to him, but there wasn't anything else he could do. At any rate, what wasn't strange in the past twenty-four hours?

When he arrived at the office, everyone was the same. However, in order to be sure, Yağmur looked at everyone one by one and said, "Good morning, friends." Now he had two seeing eyes and he immediately realized that everyone was not the same. For example, it was obvious that Selma had gone to the coiffure as soon as she got her paycheck. Curious about electronic equipment, Tayfun had a new mobile phone in his hand. Ismail's eyes were smiling. He had recently become engaged and it was apparent that he had had a good time yesterday.

He got on the internet as soon as he opened his computer and looked up the time of the Noon Prayer. It was 12:14 p.m. He would need to take his lunch break a little early. Without hesitating he said:

"Guys, I have to attend a funeral so I'll need to take my lunch break early."

---

[4] Imam.

With a worried tone of voice, Ismail said, "You have our condolences, sir! Was it someone close?"

A person could explain the degree of closeness regarding a relative, but what could he say about himself? He could only say, "He can be considered close."

At 11:32 a.m. he left the office with the condolences of all the employees. Yağmur didn't think of anything throughout the half hour drive to the graveyard. He entered through the main gate, which was the only place of passage in the high fence wall that had been made to prevent the dead from escaping or so that the living who saw the dead would not escape, and he followed the path straight to the minaret. Even in a place like this which was surrounded by dense trees, it was very easy to find the mosque by following the minaret. It was as if minarets were signs for seekers: "Salvation is here!" While getting out of his car and walking towards the place for ablutions, Yağmur could not help but look at the coffins from the corner of his eye. But the names written on them could not be seen from this distance. Actually, he didn't have the courage to go closer.

While performing ablution, his mind returned to his childhood together with the call-to-Prayer. He would hold the hand of his beloved grandfather and go to the mosque. He would prostrate together with him, open his hands in prayer and ask for a bicycle. He couldn't help but break off a piece of the warm bread they would buy from the bakery on the way home from the mosque. But now he savored neither bread nor the life he lived without his grandfather.

After the Funeral Prayer which was led by a deep-voiced *hodja*, all the funeral parties went to the courtyard to perform their last duties to the close ones they had lost. Yağmur was in the very back. Someone said, "For the adult men," the *hodja* said, "*Allahu Akbar*!" (God is the Greatest!) and all heads bowed in Prayer. Three times the *hodja* said, "Give your blessings to the deceased," and three times the crowd replied, "We did." Then they put all the coffins on the shoulders of men except for one. Yağmur shyly approached the coffin and looked at the piece of paper that had been fastened to it with a straight pin. Saying, "Maybe my misty eyes are seeing incorrectly," he wiped his tears with his hands; however, even if he did not want to believe it, his name was there: "Yağmur Sancak."

With the hope of being able to learn the truth, he immediately ran after the *hodja*.

"Hodja, who is this Yağmur Sancak? Why did you leave him here?" Yağmur asked.

"He is going to the Graveyard for the Destitute. Two workers will load the coffin on the funeral vehicle and take it to the cemetery. It's a service provided by the municipality for destitute citizens," the *hodja* replied.

Yağmur asked a logical question:

"But how do they know the name of a destitute person?"

"An anonymous good Samaritan not only registered the name of the poor man on our documents, but he even had it engraved on a tombstone and brought it to us. The tombstone is a little strange, but since it was a good deed, it couldn't be refused, of course."

While they were talking, the workers had come to the side of the coffin. Yağmur took some money out of his pocket and gave it to the workers since he wasn't comfortable with this poor fellow being sent off on his last journey like this. He asked the workers to help him carry the coffin. The *hodja* was just turning his back when Yağmur caught him by his conscience. When he said, "It's meritous, *hodja*," what could the man do? Thus, Yağmur and the *hodja* shouldered the front of the coffin and the two workers the back of it. Perhaps this was the first time a destitute person was being carried on the shoulders of others to his final journey. But Yağmur's inner ease was due more to his being able to understand what was happening than to the situation. It could be understood that all of this was the work of Servant. However, he was still uninformed about his latest act.

When the workers said, "This is it!" he saw a scene very different from the near-by graves. While the *hodja* made a prayer and the workers threw dirt onto the grave, Yağmur remained frozen like the tombstone standing before him. As the *hodja* had said, it was "a little strange." On the stone which gave no date of death, the birth date was written as "February 14, 2007." In other words, it was the day that all these strange things had begun: yesterday.

The scene that was completed when everyone had finished their job and left was much more serious, much more chilling and that much terrifying. Yağmur could not contain his tears. It seemed that the day had come that his beloved grandfather had referred to when he gave Yağmur his name: "Let a day come when he will weep like rain." The hand put on his shoulder a little later and the even softer voice were sufficient to disperse the clouds:

"Do you know why your grandfather gave you the name Yağmur?"

"..."

"Let me tell you. Just as rain is a vehicle of mercy for people, you, too, be such a vehicle for mercy that people can be saved."

Yağmur understood that finally the moment he had been waiting for had come. This was definitely him: Servant. This voice that was jolting enough to bring one to his senses; that was serene enough to make one forget all his troubles; and that was hopeful enough to make one rear up with faith—who could it belong to but him? Although he was certain of this, he was not yet ready to turn around so he asked:

"Who are you?"

"I'm Servant! Just like you."

"But I'm not a servant!"

"Don't answer without thinking. Actually, isn't everyone a servant? Don't we all serve each other? Think of an ordinary day in your life. You go to work to serve your wife; you work to serve your boss, and you pay taxes to serve your government. Let's say that you do these for a certain return; what about how you serve yourself? Aren't you aware that you serve an inner voice at every moment? It says, "I'm hungry!" and you eat. It says, "I'm thirsty!" and you drink. It says "I'm tired" and you sleep. When you want to sin, it just needs to give a command. Saying, "Immediately, sir," without giving any regard to the vileness you have fallen into, you fulfill all its commands. In other words, you're a servant, and I am Servant!" Yağmur pulled himself together, stood up and slowing turned around.

What he saw before him again made him forget to breathe: That blessed person whom he wanted to see the most in life, whom he mentioned with longing at least once a day, whom he missed fervently every moment and whom he thought was an angel when he was alive. Once when someone was relating that he had seen a white-bearded old man having a bright face in his dreams, saying, "You have seen an old man again," Yağmur had made him the subject of a joke. It was that old man. Yağmur immediately hugged him. The scent he smelled was so enchanting that he neither doubted that his grandfather had come from Paradise nor that what he lived was real.

Later he became aware of something he hadn't noticed in his amazement. The moment his tears streamed from his cheeks and fell onto his grandfather's shoulder, they evaporated. If this was due to the heat, then his hands should be hot. When he felt this strangeness, he slowly stood back. He was trying to understand what was happening. If Servant had not helped him with explanations, it was not possible to understand anything:

"I am from the Group of Servants attached to the Combatants' Unit of the Army of Good. I have been assigned especially for your training. Because you are not strong enough to see my real face, I appear as the person you love most which will make things easier for us."

"Excuse me, but I don't understand what you mean."

"We are just in the middle of a war thousands of years old that began in the heavens and is continuing on earth. This is the war between good and evil, between devils and human beings, and between Azazel and Adam. On the side of good is the Army of Good, and on the side of evil is the Army of Evil."

"The dispatching and administration of the Army of Good are executed by a council comprised of the high spirits of the Holy Sphere. Here decisions are made for necessary precautions regarding people being saved from difficulties in this world and the next. Thus, for example, agreement is made on the subject of training God's purest and most distinguished servant of the day and helping him execute his duty among others. As a necessity of this agreement, in order for the knowledge that will lead to goodness and salvation for others to be inspired in that person by means of revelation or dream, one from the Holy Sphere must appear to him and verbally speak with him. In fact, if necessary, special forces can be sent to him and other believers. All the Prophets were given duty in this way. In the application of these decisions, lower units become active, and one of these is the Messengers' Unit. It is comprised of the Prophets and angels. All revelation, inspiration and intelligence tasks are performed by this unit," said Servant.

He continued to explain in spite of Yağmur's looks of amazement:

"Another unit is the 'Protectors.' It is comprised of angels and human beings. They are responsible for protecting and supporting the other units by means of prayer or direct disposition," and added:

"Another unit is the Champions' Unit which I am a member of. Taking on more responsibility than the supportive units, it is comprised of the Prophets, saints and angels. One of its sub-divisions is the Scholars Brigade. Together with this group being comprised wholly of saints, its duty is to learn and teach all branches of knowledge necessary for being victorious in this struggle. The Combatants' Unit is comprised of 'Warriors' who fight directly with the enemy. As for the Servants' Unit..."

He continued:

"Rather than fighting with the enemy, our real duty is to save the innocent ones who are not yet from either side. Together with all the Prophets being from this unit, many angels and saints are from this unit and are working for the salvation of people. Because almost all of the struggle has piled up on our front in the present time, we have remained weak. Especially in the last century the Army of Evil has based all its tactics on us and done its best to bring over to its own side the uncommitted human beings which has made our job even more difficult. By the time we have reached one person, they have reached one thousand people and unfortunately the Servants cannot cope with such a force."

In view of these, Yağmur didn't know what to say. He just asked the first thing that came to mind:

"But why me? What do I have to do with all of this?"

"You still swallow olive pits, don't you?"

"Y...e...yes!"

"Who wanted you to do this?"

"You... I mean my grandfather."

"That grandfather that you loved so much was not just an ordinary person, Yağmur. He was one of the most faithful Servants. His care for you was not in vain; he showed you distinct attention."

"Yes, not only me, but unfortunately his other grandchildren were aware of this. Wasn't that the only reason for their jealousy?"

"Just like Jacob's love for Joseph and his other siblings' jealously. But did this stop your grandfather? No, because there was something he knew. The day would come when you, too, would become a Servant. For this reason he asked all those he knew from the Veterans' Division of the Protectors' Unit to pray for this day. They did and that day has finally arrived."

"OK, do I have to accept this," Yağmur asked, trying to understand the situation he was in.

"No, of course, there is no compulsion here. This is an offer and a matter of choice. But don't forget that being neutral will not gain you anything. Listen: One day the animals in the forest separated into two groups—the walking and the flying. Both groups wanted to be in charge of the forest. For this reason they got into a merciless fight. Only one ostrich remained neutral. Even if the walkers came and said, "Join us," he would reply, "I'm a bird. How can I join you?" If the fliers came and said, "Join us," he replied, "But I can't fly. How can I join you?" The years-long war finally ended and peace was declared. These two groups who had been merciless to one another for years embraced each other and had fun together everyday. But they never took the ostrich in. He died from loneliness. In other words, even a bird should declare his side," said Servant and continued with this example:

"You should have seen the day Abraham was going to be thrown into the fire. Nimrud had made such a fire that even birds flying hundreds of meters above were roasted and fell into the fire; for meters around the fire, the green grass yellowed and dried. A dove was seen in the sky. With just a drop of water in its beak, it flew towards the fire which all the birds had escaped from. When one of the escaping birds saw the dove flying like crazy, it asked:

'Where are you flying to like this?'

'I heard that they lit a fire and are going to throw Abraham into it. I am going to put out that fire.'

'That's fine, but are you going to put out that huge fire with one drop of water in your beak?'

'I know that the fire will not be extinguished with one drop of water, but my purpose is to declare my side.'

Don't forget! There is no place between Paradise and Hell. This road will end in one of them."

Embarrassed to look at his watch, Yağmur thought he was late and he became a little uneasy. Servant must have understood the situation for he looked up with a smile on his face and said, "Don't worry; take a look at your watch."

Yağmur couldn't believe his eyes. It was only 1:02 p.m. He remembered the Noon Prayer time on the Internet very well: 12:14 p.m. They had performed the Noon Prayer, then performed the Funeral Prayer and come here. After burying the corpse, he had talked about a half an hour with Servant, but it was still 1:02 p.m. If Servant couldn't explain this situation well, he would begin to think he was really going mad:

"Some Servants have their own unique weapons. What you are experiencing now is called 'Expansion of Time.' As if you have escaped from time, a long period of time occurs within a moment. You will see many similar events during our time together. You should prepare yourself."

"With your permission, I have a final question: How can someone like myself who has attempted every sin become a vehicle for the salvation of others?"

"I am not going to tell you that your past sins are a good thing for you. But I want you to know that you can use them for good. It is up to you to turn this situation into an advantage. In this situation you know very well why people sin, what they think of before and after they sin, and the Army of Evil's means of attraction. Plus this is not just dry knowledge; it is things you learned from experience by living them. In this case, you will understand well the language, state and difficulties of many who have not yet joined the Army of Evil. Also you, too, know that, except for the Prophets, there is no sinless person. Maybe there are those who think they are sinless, but they have the disease of condescending to those they determine to be sinners. Succeeding in this duty you will take on is an impossible task for them. For the secret of this job is to be a human among humans. Learning what is necessary to perform your duty is much easier than understanding all of this. And I would like to give you the good tidings that, with special permission I got from my superiors, everything I will teach, you will learn by personally experiencing it."

This greatly surprised Yağmur:

"What do you mean?"

This will be the place where we meet for our daily training. Every day you will perform the Noon Prayer at the cemetery mosque and then come to this grave. Don't wear a watch. You will close your eyes while pronouncing the *Basmala*[5] before reciting the chapter Al-Fatiha and open them when you say 'Amen.' This grave will be a door for your passage to another realm. Actually that is true for everyone! But now I would like to warn you that regardless of

---

[5] In the Name of God, the All-Merciful, the All-Compassionate.

what you see when you open your eyes, do not be afraid and do not close your eyes."

Yağmur was already frightened:

"Do I have to see everything? Can't you just explain things like you did today?"

"You are right to worry. But you should know that certainty has three degrees. They are: Certainty of Knowledge, Certainty of Observation, and Certainty of Experience. The Prophets knew everything from Certainty of Experience. For example, the things taught to our blessed Prophet during the Night Journey. Even if I explained this, it would be difficult for you to understand it. Certainty of Knowledge is knowing something only on the level of knowledge; most scholars are from this group. Learning by listening to me can only be Certainty of Knowledge. Certainty of Observation is stronger than that. Can a person's explaining what he heard ever be the same as explaining what he experienced? You are going to learn everything by living it. Only if you believe in this way, will it be easier for you to help others. Such a belief will be your strongest support for constancy on this path of powerful service. Only because the Prophets believed in their truths on the level of Certainty of Experience were they able to represent their beliefs, and they never took a step backwards."

"With your permission, I will go now. I am curious about the answers to so many questions that they won't all fit in one day," Yağmur said.

"Don't forget! At this moment we are in "Expanded Time." If we want, we can begin and finish all the training. However, it's better to learn piece by piece in order to assimilate the knowledge. Isn't it easier to digest food when it is eaten bite by bite?"

Yağmur acted immediately and tried to kiss his hand. This was a habit from his childhood. He would never leave his grandfather without kissing his hand and receiving his beneficial prayer. However, Servant did not permit this:

"Don't forget! I am a Servant. I am here to serve you. Soon you will be a Servant too. And throughout your life of service you will never have others kiss your hand!"

Saying, "As you like, sir; please forgive my faults," Yağmur withdrew.

Now he was one of those who knew the other side. What remained was to show this. This tree-lined cemetery road that he was walking on now would take him to Paradise and when he arrived there, he would be happy because of the many people following him rather than the blessings he would meet there. For this road was the path of the Servants...

## The Journey Begins

That evening when he arrived at home, Yağmur was beside himself. He was enveloped by an indescribable excitement in regard to what he would experience the next day. Rehnüma must have been aware of this for she was trying to understand what was going on by asking one question after another. However, Yağmur thought that he shouldn't tell anyone about this training. For according to him, the things that were happening were not the kinds of things that could be understood without experiencing them.

He thought to himself, "I have to make preparations for the journey. But preparation for such a journey should be at least as distinct as the journey."

When he asked Rehnüma, "Do you know where the old books from my grandfather are," he received an answer that showed his years of heedlessness:

"You can look in the depot where we keep things we don't need."

"You mean the coal depot?"

"Didn't you say, 'These are unnecessary'? I didn't even look at the box!"

He had never been so embarrassed. How had he thrown the only keepsake from his dear grandfather into a corner of the coal depot? Those books were his grandfather's most valuable and only treasure; he had not been able to think of selling them even during the hardest of times. Hadn't he entrusted them to Yağmur rather than his other grandchildren because he would value them?

Red-faced from his embarrassment, he went down to the coal depot and felt the joy of finding a treasure when he saw the books. He grabbed the box containing everything that remained from his grandfather and ran back to his home. He went to the cold living room which was the only place he could remain alone and excitedly opened the dusty box.

Now these things before him had a distinct value in his eyes. These were the sacred trusts of one of the most faithful Servants from the Servants' Unit. There was a prayer bead with ninety-nine beads on the top of the box's contents. He picked up the ninety-nine beads, for each of which he wanted to shed a tear. The reason for this was not only because he remembered the days when the beads were in his grandfather's hand, but at the same time because of the scent that spread throughout the living room. It was the same scent he smelled today when he embraced Servant. He took the book on top and, after holding it to his heart, he opened a page randomly without looking. Everything he needed for the journey was here:

"Rebuild what you have destroyed. Clean what you have sullied. Turn your evil into good. Polish your being that has become darkened with sin. Return what you took to its owner. You escaped from your Master; you fell remote from your servanthood to Him. Immediately turn to Him and repent."

He looked at the cover of the book: it read "*Fathu'r-Rabbani* by Abdulqadr al-Jilani." He said, "My God! Be pleased with this great person!" and he walked with determined steps to the bathroom to make a full ablution. He wanted to be cleansed from all the sins he had committed until now. Just as a person doesn't load himself down with unnecessary things on a trip, he was determined to leave behind that load of sins on his back and set out upon his journey like that. As he asked for forgiveness with his most sincere and heartfelt pleas, he held his tears as witnesses to this. Then performing the Night Prayer, he went to bed. This time it wasn't necessary for him to toss and turn a half an hour in bed before being able to fall asleep. Because now there was a long path to travel and a Morning Prayer to get up for.

When Rehnüma woke up for the Morning Prayer, she became worried when she didn't see her husband in bed. She had become so accustomed to getting up for Prayer every morning and watching him sleep. Even though this upset her a lot, she believed that one day this would change. She suddenly became hopeful and, jumping out of bed, she began to look for him. An indistinct voice could be heard from the living room. She slowly opened the door and found Yağmur murmuring some things on the Prayer rug. At that moment she became exulted. What a tremendous thing it was to see that the prayers she had made for years were accepted. In order not to disturb him, she carefully closed the door and went to take ablution.

Without being bothered by the coldness of the living room, Yağmur pleaded for minutes. What made him cry until his eyes had swollen was not the sorrow regarding his past mistakes, but the breadth of God's mercy. When he raised his head from the Prayer rug, it was just getting light outside. Now not just a new day, but a new life was dawning for him.

With a smile on both their faces as a reflection of the peace in their hearts, they had breakfast together for the first time in a long time. After forty-five minutes of cheerful conversation and while Rehnüma had not yet learned the reason for this sudden change, Yağmur immediately got up with the excuse of being late.

Now his view of his friends at work had also changed. He was thinking about what Servant had explained and he wanted to do something for them. But he didn't know where to start or how to do it, and he thought that he should be patient until his training was complete.

He left at 11:45 a.m. to be on time for the Friday Prayer and he arrived at the mosque at the cemetery just as the call-to-Prayer was about to finish. The courtyard was again full or lined-up coffins and people with sunglasses. Thinking that this trend came from the West, he thought it must be due to the instinct to ignore death. However, the eye of death was darker than these sunglasses. After the Prayer led by the deep-voiced *hodja*, he went to the head of his grave.

Even coming every day to see his own grave was enough to explain the meaning of life. Was it possible to not think about death and the beyond after seeing this scene. Without losing time, he mentally repeated what Servant had said. Everything was on track. Since he didn't have his watch on, he could now begin. With excitement mixed with fear, Yağmur closed his eyes. After reciting the *Basmala*, he repeated the chapter Al-Fatiha word by word and...

# The Place Where Everything Began

The scene he saw was magnificent. Every place was full of prostrating angels for as far as he could see. Two exceptional figures facing one another in this fantastic tableau immediately caught his attention, and Servant appeared at his side:

"The one in the exact middle is God's vicegerent, the father of mankind and the first Prophet, Adam. The one standing among the angels who are shaking from fear even though they are prostrating is one of the prominent jinni, the rebellious Iblis. Or with his special name, Azazel... A little earlier God had commanded all the angels, including Azazel, to bow before Adam. Azazel's disobedience and God's wrath frightened the angels so much that they were shaking due to the possibility of His crushing everyone. God asked Azazel, 'What prevented you from bowing down to this human being whom I personally created? Did you want to act proudly or have you become exalted?' Listen to the response of Azazel filled with pride, envy and rebellion: 'I am better than him. For You created me from fire and him from mud. How can I bow down to someone created from mud?'"

Yağmur couldn't believe his ears. Saying, "This cannot be the reason for such great rebellion," he couldn't hide his amazement.

"Of course, this is not the only reason," Servant affirmed. "Although Azazel was created differently from the angels, his love for God was so great that with his centuries of effort, he was exalted to be among the angels. He believed he had such a unique place before God that he was not able to accept a human being created from simple clay to be more exalted and loved in God's presence. In his own view he had lost his throne to Adam. But actually if he had been sincere in this love, he would have obeyed God's command without any hesitation. As can be understood from his not bowing, Azazel's love was egotistical."

Servant continued with his helpful explanations:

"In addition, his present rebellion is not a spontaneous revolt; it was planned before to be made just at the right time. For before Adam was created, God had said that he would create a vicegerent. The angels asked, 'Are you going to create someone who will make corruption on earth and spill blood?' This 'vicegerent' title used for man was sufficient for Azazel to consume himself with anxiety. While talking with some angels, he said, 'I have been performing worship for a long time without resting; is he going to be superior to me as soon as he is created? I swear I will not accept this!' He had long since made his decision. The current rebellion is nothing other than the fruit of his sins of rebellion, pride and envy."

Even from this distance, Yağmur could see the fire of enmity in Azazel's eyes. This had frightened him so much that he used all his power not to close his eyes. Squeezing with all his might, Yağmur was holding onto Servant's arm for support. Servant continued to explain:

"God drove out Azazel saying, 'Then leave here! You have been expelled. Undoubtedly damnation will dwell over you until the day of punishment!' Azazel is looking for a way out. However, instead of asking for forgiveness and bowing down, he plans to get revenge from Adam.

At that moment Azazel began to speak like a bankrupt one who has played his last card:

'O my Lord! Grant me respite till the Day when they are raised from the dead!'

He began speaking like this, but his speech turned into a challenge: 'If you allow me to live until the Last Day, I swear I will bind most of his progeny to me.'

Even if he didn't get what he fully wished for, Azazel was pleased with getting a respite until the Resurrection. He didn't refrain from hurling threats to intimidate Adam whom he saw as his enemy: 'I swear to your Majesty, I will lead a certain number of your servants into deviation. Since You sentenced me to mischief, I swear I will consequently set a trap for them on Your path; I also swear that then I will bother them from their front, back, right and left. Thus, You will find most of them to be ungrateful to You!'"

Yağmur didn't know what to say. What audacity, what rebellion, what hatred this was. What wouldn't this devil, who could become so aggressive even in the presence of God who had created him from nothing, do to human beings whom he had taken as enemies? Yağmur became very frightened. He wanted to get away as fast as possible. He even forgot about Servant who had stood beside him while all this was going on. When he turned around, they came eye-to-eye with each other.

With his smile that inspired tranquility, Servant again began to explain:

"Wait a second; calm down! When you hear the response God gave him, you'll feel much better. God said, 'Use your voice to move them internally as much as you have the power to; become partners to their goods and children; make promises to them... But what can a devil promise but deceit? I have some true servants; you have no dominion over them. Their Lord suffices them as attorney before your deceits against them.' You're aware, too, that Adam has no responsibility in this enmity. His only crime was to be loved and chosen by God. In this case, Azazel's real enemy is the chooser and not the chosen. However, because it is impossible to make an enemy of the Creator of the created, Azazel turned his gaze directly to Adam and his progeny. With his horsemen and foot soldiers, which we called the Army of Evil, he will enter a relentless war with all of mankind. Before such an enemy that is much more powerful and hateful than man, God has said that He is your attorney and He wants you to feel that He is always at your side."

"There's something I don't understand," Yağmur said. "Why does God allow such a rebel to bother people? Couldn't He destroy him now if He wanted?"

"Of course, All-Powerful God could immediately smash Azazel if He wanted to. But think about why He created man, jinni and angels. He was an unknown treasure. He was the possessor of undefiable power, inimitable art and unattainable knowledge. He wanted to be known and to be praised, celebrated, affirmed and professed as One. Because the angels He created are without will, their worship is remote from any choice. They have no choice but to bow down and fulfill His commands. Because of this there is no prohibition they have to observe. The true meaning of servanthood can only be found in human beings."

"For man would be left free to serve or not serve Him, and by restraining himself from prohibited things and obeying difficult commands, he will praise, celebrate, affirm and profess Him to be One."

Servant continued his explanations:

"Just at this point Azazel comes in. He will start a fire of desire in man for all prohibitions God made to human beings. It is Azazel who turns people from their intentions with various misgivings just when they have decided to obey God's commands. Thus, he can drag people he has turned away from the path of servanthood to the torment that awaits him. As I told you before, we Servants took an oath to save people from his traps and we try with all our might to destroy these games of Azazel. I say 'games' because this struggle has its own rules which have been determined by God in whose every work there is wisdom. Even He, as a necessity of these rules, did not destroy Azazel a little earlier and gave him permission to attack human beings. In this case, Azazel and his army and us have to act according to these laws. Otherwise, what we call 'the secret of being tested' or the wisdom of human beings coming to this world would be lost, but God does not permit this."

Now Yağmur knew much better how dangerous the devil is. He saw in a flash with his own eyes how a war against mankind began that would continue for thousands of years, even at the cost of God's condemnation. When he looked at Adam, he saw not a person who would "make corruption on the earth and spill blood," but a pure human being who had no goal but to serve God with every atom in his being, but, at the same time, who had gained the enmity of the greatest evil in existence. This meant that Azazel would have a role in the corruption that would appear on earth and in every drop of blood that would be spilled.

Just at that moment Servant asked a very interesting question:

"Would you like to see Paradise?"

Yağmur's astonishment was obvious in his reply:

"I don't understand; which Paradise?"

"The Paradise in which God placed Adam and Eve saying, 'O Adam, Satan is definitely the enemy of you and your wife. Consequently, do not allow him to remove you from Paradise. At that time you will fall into difficulty.' Shortly you will witness Azazel's first victory in this war. Go closer and close your eyes," Servant said. Then he opened his broad white cloak with strange embroidery on it and wrapped it around Yağmur.

The moment Yağmur closed his eyes, he felt very strange things—like rising by falling, turning by standing still, and freezing by burning. Just as these seem impossible, describing what he felt at that moment was impossible. When Servant said, "Open your eyes," he did so enthusiastically.

When what man can see, feel, know and speak are this limited, how can he express infinite beauty—even only what he can perceive—with limited language and limited words? While he was only trying to see the scene in front of his dazzled eyes, Servant said:

"Look at this side. What you see is Adam and his wife—two blessed people whom God had made all of Paradise permissible to except for one tree. As you recall, I mentioned that there is no test for angels because they do not have the right of choice. But this is not the case for human beings. There must be one prohibition among this many blessings so that God can see if they obey it or not. In other words, shortly both will be subject to a great test. You saw with your own eyes how Azazel failed his first test with Adam. Let's see what man does in his first test with Azazel."

On the one hand, Yağmur was listening to Servant and, on the other hand, he couldn't take his eyes off Azazel who was pacing back and forth. It was obvious from his mental state that he had a devilish plan. When he saw that the opportunity he was looking for had come, he immediately gathered himself together and in spite of all the hatred in him, he called out in a friendly manner to Adam and Eve who were passing close by him:

"Why don't you eat from the fruit of this tree?"

"God prohibited us from eating the fruit of that tree. In fact, even our approaching it has been forbidden."

"But the tree is beautiful and the taste of its fruit is unequaled in Paradise. No one has eaten a sweeter fruit than this. I don't think you will be able to eat sweeter fruit than this."

"Anyway, we partake of all of the blessings of Paradise as much as we want."

"Well, do you know why you were prohibited from approaching this tree?"

"No, we don't know why."

"It's because if you eat from the fruit of this tree, you will become angels and you will stay in Paradise forever."

"Are you speaking the truth? ... You're not fooling us, are you?"

"I swear in the Name of God that I wish the best for you. What gain could I have from this?"

Then Azazel sighed and continued:

"I feel sorry for you. Your short will end one day later and you will be gone. The blessings of Paradise will remain. What would be lost if you ate and drank in immortal life in Paradise? If I were in your place, I wouldn't miss this opportunity. Plus, what will happen if you just eat one time? After God has valued you enough to make all the angels bow down before you, He won't mind your eating just one piece of fruit!"

Adam and Eve liked the idea of staying in Paradise eternally. As they were reaching for the fruit, Yağmur said, "I don't believe it. Although God warned them openly about Azazel, how can they do this?" He didn't think of his own sins while he was saying this.

"As you see," Servant said, "this is not just Azazel's victory over Adam and Eve; it is the victory of the devil over man, the victory of evil over good, and the victory of the Army of Evil over the Army of Good. This first victory gave Azazel such a boost that he has absolutely no doubt that he can fool all men until Doomsday. Now this relentless war will continue on earth due to their being thrown out of Paradise as enemies to each other by God's command."

"Then are we going to earth now?" Yağmur asked curiously.

Servant replied:

"Yes, but to your gravesite. This is enough for today. Tomorrow we will watch together the struggle given at different times by the Army of Good after its first defeat by its greatest enemy. Now close your eyes and after reciting the *Basmala*, In the Name of God, and then the chapter An-Nas. When it is finished, you can open your eyes.

In addition, I want to warn you about something. The intelligence units of the Army of Evil are aware of you and they informed their commander Azazel about you. I want you to be much more careful after this. They will attack you at every opportunity. If you suspect a possible attack, immediately read this chapter. Reinforcements from the Protectors' Unit will be at your side to help you."

As always Yağmur put his curiosity before his fear: "How do you know this?"

"When we first met, I mentioned the Messengers' Unit. The intelligence division of this unit works much faster than that of the Army of Evil, and it has never been seen that they gave incorrect information. Go now and in case of an encounter with the enemy, don't lose your composure; just remember what I said!"

Yağmur did what he was told and when he opened his eyes, he found himself at the head of his grave. Now he understood much better what kind of enemy he was up against:

"I am amazed that Adam ate that fruit, but what should I say about the sins I have made throughout my life? He only complied with the devil once in his life and he lost his heavenly homeland. What about me? Who knows how many times I have believed that rebel until now and obeyed the commands of that accursed creature at the expense of God's prohibitions? God said, 'Get up!' but I was consoled with the devil's lullabies. God said, 'Don't break any hearts!' but the devil held and I hit. God said,

'Stay away from the forbidden things!' but I set the devil's table. If I had not heard what my grandfather said, I might have no hope for mercy. But is that possible? How beautifully he put it: 'What are your sins in comparison with His mercy? It is enough for you to repent. He will forgive you immediately. Just so you are one of the repenters, my sweetheart.' May God have mercy on me and you, dear grandfather."

# Two Armies on Earth

Yağmur was on edge all day long. Because he didn't know when, from which side, and how the enemy was going to attack, he constantly recited the chapter An-Nas. He thought to himself, "It would be great if there was a way I could see the enemy."

When he remembered that Adam had made a mistake even though he was able to see Azazel, he thought, "I guess this wouldn't help either. The devil is so clever that he would find a way to fool me. In addition, how do I know I haven't seen him from time to time? At the end of the chapter An-Nas which I constantly read, it says that the devil can be from jinni and human beings too. Also as far as I know, jinni can enter the shape of humans, animals and even inanimate creatures." Getting caught up in the feeling that he was surrounded by enemies, Yağmur recited the chapter An-Nas again, but without losing his composure.

At that moment the conversations of his friends at the office got his attention. Tayfun was trying to convince Ismail of something:

"Look, a few months later you have a wedding coming up. Is it easy to get married? You will have a lot of expenses. Come and play lotto! What will you lose?"

"Forget these, Brother Tayfun. Who has won until now so that I can win? It's not the money I gave; but when it doesn't happen, you feel really bad."

"Oh, this is too much, huh! OK, no one has won for four weeks, but that's even better. Do you know how much the accumulated prize will be this week? A full one million, two-hundred thousand liras. Imagine if you win. You have a good heart; I know you will win. Then I guess you will give me a treat."

"OK! Give me a few. Otherwise, it's obvious that I can't escape your tongue."

Yağmur was very surprised by what he heard. Although he had heard similar dialogues many times before, this was the first time it sounded so odd to him. For while he was listening to them, the talk between Adam and Azazel came alive before his eyes. Could they be this similar? He had not intervened before, but now he couldn't restrain himself. As a Servant he gathered his courage and turned towards Ismail and said:

"Ismail I think you are right in what you said. I have never seen anyone who won money from lotto. In addition, as you said, when your expectations are not met, you will be disappointed for nothing. In my opinion, it's best for you not to play."

Although he was very surprised by this unexpected intervention, it was obvious that Ismail was happy in every way:

"You're right, sir! I didn't really want to play. I was going to play only not to offend Brother Tayfun. Thank you very much," Ismail said and sat back down in his chair again.

Yağmur felt like he was going to burst. He guessed that very few things in his life so far had made him that pleased. Even though he was aware of Tayfun's situation, he was not going to forego the satisfaction of having done his duty as a Servant. He saw himself as a hero who had saved an innocent victim before a hungry lion. And he felt brave enough to tangle with lions for the sake of all innocent victims... After this life would have meaning and he wanted to serve people like this as much as he wanted to breathe.

Again he left a little early in order to reach the Noon Prayer. Not putting his uneasiness into words a little earlier, Tayfun didn't miss the opportunity to say in a suggestive way:

"Sir, you're leaving early again. Hopefully it's for a good cause."

Yağmur shut Tayfun up with an intimidating answer:

"If the General Manager asks, have him call me on my cell phone!"

It was obvious that in the near future Tayfun would make trouble, but with the answer he just gave, he showed both Tayfun and himself what he could risk. Either he would lie and accept the devil as his advocate or not abandon the truth and take God as his advocate. He headed towards the cemetery with the contentment of having done the right thing.

His coming to the same cemetery for three days caused him to see himself like one of its inhabitants. Again the coffins and the families of the deceased were waiting in the courtyard; they had taken their places like different actors enlivening the same scene. They were waiting for the *hodja*, who played the same role everyday, to finish his work and come.

After the Prayer, Yağmur came to the head of his grave without losing time. After he closed his eyes and said, "Amen," he again opened his eyes: He saw hills of sand wherever he looked. It was in a very hot and dry place. A vague activity far away caught his attention. Just as he was turning towards it, he heard Servant's voice:

"What you see in the distance is Adam and his family of forty-two. Come! Let's walk, and I'll tell you what's happening,"

Servant continued:

"After Adam and Eve were sent down to earth, they found each other—after a long search—at the hill called the Mount of Mercy near by. Then they settled here and made a family. Eve gave birth to twins—one girl and one boy—twenty times and thus they had forty children. Meanwhile Adam was busy with farming in order to take care of his family. Most importantly, he was informed by an ambassador sent to him from the Holy Sphere, with a ten-page composition, the precautions that must be taken against the devil and the Army of Evil. Consequently, he took the title of the first Prophet."

Meanwhile they had drawn close enough for their eyes to clearly distinguish, and Servant continued his explanations:

"The one carrying crops on his back is Adam's oldest son Cain. He farms like his father. Look, a little farther away is Able returning from grazing his animals. The male from Eve's second birth, Able, is busy with animal husbandry. The whole family is busy with wedding preparations. They will cross marry the first twins with the second twins. In other words, Cain will marry Able's twin Jumella and Able will marry Cain's twin Aclima."

Yağmur expressed his pessimism:

"Only I think there is a problem. It seems as if there will shortly be a war, not a wedding. Look at Cain's face and how he arched his eyebrows and ground his teeth when he saw that Able had come. If you didn't explain it, I would have thought that they are enemies, not brothers."

"It would not be incorrect to call them enemies. It cannot be said that Cain is very happy about this decision of Adam's. He is determined to marry his own twin Aclima. Regardless of how much his father and mother give advice, he prefers to listen to someone else."

Yağmur was immediately curious:

"Who is that?"

"Let's look carefully around us. Can you see a familiar face?" Servant asked.

Yağmur looked at everyone's face carefully one-by-one, and he saw Azazel mixed in the crowd like a wolf among some sheep. When Azazel saw Able was approaching, he immediately drew close to Cain and said:

"Look at him! How haughty he is. He is going to take your beloved Aclima from your hands; that's why he's so arrogant."

"Let him be happy for now. If he thinks I am going to allow this, he is mistaken. He will never be able to take Aclima from me," Cain asserted.

Azazel continued speaking: "In this case, it is necessary to do something immediately. Otherwise it will be too late and your right will be taken from you. You know that your father loves him more than he loves you. Maybe he concocted this cross marriage just because Able loves Aclima. Maybe he just wants to hurt you."

Cain said, "It's true. He is not aware of that devilishness behind that innocent face. His love has blinded him. He does not see what a hypocrite he is. Only I can stand up to him."

Cain walked towards Able. Azazel stood back and was watching them with delight. His laughter resounded so loudly in Yağmur's ears that he had to hold his hands over his ears. It was as if a strange animal was screaming with feelings between pain and lust.

Seeing Cain and Able from the door of his tent just as they were about to square off, Adam called out:

"Cain! Able! Both of you come here."

Yağmur immediately went to the door of the tent to listen to what was being said.

"Look," Adam said, "there is a Divine solution to this disagreement between the two of you. Both of you are going to make a sacrifice for God. The owner of whichever sacrifice is accepted and burned by a fire coming from the sky will marry Aclima."

"However you like, dear father," said Able, reflecting his full respect and surrender.

Cain also accepted this idea and said, "So be it."

...

They left the tent. While Yağmur ran after Able, Azazel followed Cain. When Able reached his flock, an angel drew close and said, "Present the best and most valuable among these animals as a sacrifice to God tomorrow."

Able was very pleased with this inspiration; it was obvious from the smile on his face. Thus, for the first time Yağmur saw an angel on duty from the Messengers' Unit giving inspiration.

On the other hand, Azazel continued to advise Cain:

"You know that you have a right to Aclima. Don't say you're going to give a large part of your crops as a sacrifice as well. It is going to be burned anyway. A handful of wheat is enough. At any rate you are going to get Aclima; don't lose that much wheat for nothing!"

"That's right," Cain said. "If I sacrifice this much wheat, it's enough! Our Lord, the owner of Paradise that my father described does not need my wheat!"

Servant came to Yağmur's side. While Yağmur excitedly explained how a little earlier an angel had given inspiration to Able, Servant said, "Angels only want what is good for people. According to the information that angel received, that was the best thing for Able. This is true for everyone. A person's 'inner voice' will always whisper what is best for him. Just as Able did not see that angel, other people do not see them either, but they definitely hear their voices. For their Conscience translates what it has heard. I'm going to show you step-by-step how all this mechanism works. But come closer now and close your eyes! Let's see which sacrifice will be accepted."

...

They stood on the side and curiously began to watch what would happen. Cain came forth and put the bunch of wheat stalks he had brought and retreated. Able, on the other hand, left his best sheep and courteously returned to his place. Adam was there as a witness. Azazel was waiting curiously at Cain's side.

The awaited fire came and accepted Able's sacrifice. Azazel breathed a sigh of relief. The sacrifice of his student, whom he advised, not being accepted meant that everything was going as planned, and he felt much more relaxed.

When Cain left with a fury, Azazel followed him:

"It was obvious this would happen. They try everything to take your right. You don't have to accept this. Think a minute; who is the source of all this?"

"Who? Able, of course!"

"In this case, if you remove the source, the problem will go away. If you want Aclima, you don't have any other choice."

"That's right. There is only one way to prevent this marriage, and that is to eliminate Able. Then Aclima will be mine."

Not much time had passed after this conversation between Azazel and Cain when Cain spilled the blood of his guiltless, innocent brother Able—plus he did it to the accompaniment of Azazel's laughter.

Yağmur was so upset by this scene that he held on to Servant and with looks expressing that he wanted to leave, he didn't take his eyes off Servant. In no way could he have turned around and looked at that innocent blood. However, he was unaware of how much innocent blood he would see throughout this journey.

When Servant saw Yağmur's angry looks due to Azazel's two consecutive victories, he couldn't help but say:

"It's time for you to relax a little. Azazel will not win every battle! There are many humans who know how to put him in his place. Would you like to see?"

"Of course," Yağmur replied. "I would really like to! Otherwise I am going to lose my desire to fight against the Army of Evil."

"Then let's not lose any time. Immediately close your eyes..."

# Devils Cry Too

When Yağmur opened his eyes, the surroundings looked very familiar.

These places resembled the places where Adam and his family lived. Servant began to explain the puzzle regarding what was passing through Yağmur's mind:

"Yes, these lands are where Adam and his family lived. Look carefully at this side. The empty space in the middle is just where Abraham and his son Ishmael will, with God's command, place the sacred Ka'ba. If we wait here, we will see Abraham who will build it."

"He is traveling a road approximately a thousand kilometers long to sacrifice his only son. They are about to arrive," Servant said. He was expecting Yağmur's question:

"I didn't understand. What do you mean 'sacrifice'? Is his son Ishmael at fault?"

"No! To the contrary, he is the most obedient and respectful son in human history and he loved his father enough to die for him. However, before setting out on this road, Abraham saw the same dream three nights in a row. He had no doubt that it was God's command for him to sacrifice his son. This was one of the biggest tests he faced.

Let's see what Abraham, who didn't listen to the devil when he was going to be thrown in the fire, will do this time," Servant said.

Then he made a very interesting offer:

"Would you like to see what is happening in the Army of Evil's headquarters at this moment?"

"Won't that be very dangerous? We will go among all those devils. What if they see us?" Yağmur asked.

"Don't worry," Servant said, "just don't forget what I told you before!"

Yağmur knew very well what he should do in this situation. He immediately drew close to Servant and closed his eyes. When he opened his eyes after that strange feeling he had become accustomed to, his surroundings were filled with devils. He had never seen such ugly creatures in his life. It was a scene not even to be found in the most horrible films. There was an abominable smell in the air. Even if none of the devils could see them, Yağmur was afraid of taking a breath. He wasn't even aware that he had taken a step backwards from Servant.

Someone came in who was at least as disgusting and terrible as the others. He stopped in front of Azazel who was sitting behind a desk and, bowing down, he gave the greeting:

"May you be damned, Master."

When Azazel said, "What is it, accursed one?" he began to explain with fervor:

"Our Master, news has just come from our spies in Egypt. Abraham has set out for Mecca to sacrifice his son to God. Uhh..."

"Don't beat around the bush, stupid! Say what you are going to say."

"I am afraid you will get angry, but... He is about to reach Mecca. Our troops were a little slow again. Forgive us, Master!"

"What suffering you have caused me, accursed ones. It just takes a second to come here from Egypt. Immediately catch those clumsy ones and throw them into prison. I'll take care of them as soon as I finish my work with Abraham."

"Shall we immediately send the Special Forces, Master?"

"Don't be ridiculous, accursed one! What have you done right so far that you can handle Abraham. Abraham... Abraham... You don't know him. Until now I have never been able to handle him in any of our encounters. He has dedicated himself to God so much that it's impossible to understand it. I was very hopeful when he was going to be thrown into the fire. We had made a good job that day with Nimrud. Even while a torture that could be related until Doomsday was awaiting him, we weren't able to make him stray from his path. But now I have a good opportunity. When he got a son like Ishmael after not having a child for years, his joy was complete. In fact, he loved him so much that I understood then that one day

God would test him with his son. The opportunity I have been awaiting for years has finally arrived. Let's see, Abraham, how you are going to escape from my hands now... Hurry up and get my 'Man from Mecca' clothing ready!"

"At your command, Accursed Master!"

"Wait a minute... Do you smell something? It's as if there is someone here..."

What Yağmur had been afraid of was happening. Azazel got up from his desk and, smelling and looking around, he began to walk around the room. Yağmur held his breath. As Azazel was approaching him, he slowly began to back away.

Azazel said to his men:

"Hurry and close the doors."

Yağmur didn't know what to do. He was aware that Servant had gone away from his side and he wanted to go towards him. But Azazel was headed straight towards him. The moment he felt Azazel's breath that smelled like the soot of Hell on his sweaty face, that was the moment he forgot everything. He did what any ordinary person would do: he closed his eyes. This was what Servant had especially warned him not to do, and unfortunately he did it. He closed his eyes. But nothing changed. He still saw that ugliness that he didn't want to see. Even worse, Azazel could see him too.

As soon as merciless Azazel saw Yağmur, he put his claws around his neck. Just as Yağmur had difficulty breathing, at the same time he felt a fire enveloping his whole body. Azazel came close to his ear and whispered like a snake:

"Who are you?"

"I am Servant."

"Ha, ha, ha... In that case, serve me!"

"No, never!

Azazel's laughter was so unbearable that, on the one hand, Yağmur was afraid he was going to lose his mind and, on the other hand, he was looking around with the hope of seeing Servant.

Azazel continued to spew poison:

"Don't look around in vain. Your friend left long ago. Now you are alone. If you accept what I say, I will make you very comfortable. Houses, cars, fame, position—whatever you want is in the palm of my hand."

While Azazel was listing all of these, each one was passing in front of Yağmur's eyes. The terraced house of his dreams, the car he had wanted to buy for a long time, the position of general manager of the firm he worked for, his grandfather... Yes, he could choose all of these. He wasn't sure; maybe it was Servant appearing in his grandfather's form. Remembering Servant, Yağmur slowly began to come to his senses.

He remembered what he was supposed to do in case of an enemy attack:

"*A'udhu billahi min ash-shaytanirrajim. Bismillahir-Rahmanir-Rahim* (I seek refuge in God from Satan eternally rejected from God's Mercy. In the Name of God, the All-Merciful, the All-Compassionate).

*Qul audhu bi Rabbinnas* (Say: I seek refuge in the Lord of humankind) ..."

Without even the chapter being completed, the voices of an approaching crowd were heard: "*Allahu Akbar*!" As if an earthquake were occurring, everyplace was shaking and all the devils were fleeing left and right.

When an excited devil came and said:

"The Combatants' Unit is coming, sir," Azazel let go of Yağmur and saying:

"I have to catch up with Abraham! Look out for yourselves, you dirty accursed ones," he left. The devil must have been as astonished as Yağmur for without taking another breath, he died by means of a deep blue sword in Servant's hand.

Servant looked at Yağmur with all his compassion and was only able to say:

"Just in time."

Then taking Yağmur's hand, he added:

"We're late. We have to go immediately."

Of course, Yağmur knew what he had to do.

...

When he opened his eyes, Azazel, dressed in the clothing of an old man, was about to meet Abraham at the entrance to Mecca.

"Hey Abraham, where are you going like this?" he said.

"I have some work in this valley."

"Hey Abraham, tell me. If the devil appears in a person's dream and orders him to strangle his son, should that command be obeyed?"

Abraham recognized him.

"Get out of here, you accursed creature. What I saw was definitely my Lord's command. Get out of my way," he said and continued on.

Azazel's state was worthy of watching. This time before him it was Abraham whom God called "My friend," and by whom he had always been humiliated although he had encountered Abraham many times. Azazel thought to himself:

"It isn't necessary to push my luck here; Abraham is not an easy bite. I need someone less experienced. But who? Let me see... let me see... I've found it! I can go to Hagar." Azazel jumped for joy.

...

Yağmur and Servant were crouched in a corner; they stood behind Azazel who was eyeing his prey. At that moment Abraham said to his beloved son Ishmael who was about to reach puberty:

"Son, find a rope and knife and follow me."

Ishmael was so adorable that the idea of sacrificing this child, who was the most beautiful child he had ever seen, made even Yağmur think long and hard.

They followed Azazel closely. The greatest enemy of man approached Hagar and asked:

"Hey Hagar, where did Abraham go?"

"As far as I know, they went to gather wood."

"Now I really feel sorry for you, Hagar. Did you know that your husband Abraham came to sacrifice your son Ishmael? Whether you believe it or not, a little later he is going to cut his throat."

"What are you saying, man? Abraham is a very merciful and soft-hearted father. He loves Ishmael very much. He would never do such a thing. Would a father kill his only son?"

"Poor you, Hagar! Didn't he once leave you in the middle of the desert alone as prey for wild animals?"

"He acted according to God's command then. If God had not commanded it, he would never have done such a thing."

Azazel had brought the conversation just to the point he wanted to:

"That's it!. Now he is going to cut your son's throat with God's command..."

When Hagar had stayed alone in the land years earlier, she had proven her faith by saying, "For certain God will not forsake us!" Proving this faith again she said:

"If God has commanded this, then of course he should do it. What befalls us is to surrender to His commands."

Not getting any results from his first sally, Azazel, changing tactics, wanted to manipulate Hagar from her motherly feelings:

"That's fine, Hagar, but don't you have any mercy towards your child? What kind of mother are you? How can you willingly surrender your son to a knife? What kind of heart do you have that accepts such a thing?"

"Look stranger! Only God can grant him to us. If He wants his sacrifice, then that is our duty. If He wants it, we will also be sacrifices after our son."

Azazel was squeezed into a corner. There was only one way left. He had to take this risk even if it meant denying himself:

"Are you aware of what you said? Abraham is going to cut your son's throat because he was fooled by a devil he saw in his dream. Run and stop him! Should a child be sacrificed for the sake of a dream?"

Having become ridiculous and inconsistent, Azazel's trickery had become apparent. Hagar looked at the man a little more carefully. Saying, "You can only be a devil. Now get out of here! My God, keep us from this evil," she drove him off.

Yağmur could not hide his amazement before what he had seen and he said:

"If I had been in her place, I would have long since been fooled by Azazel. What faith and what surrender!"

Meanwhile Azazel, with his head down, went farther and farther away mumbling to himself:

"How much I have suffered from this family! Hagar is just like her husband. She defeats me every time. What dreams I had come here with. When Hagar heard what I had to say, she should have jumped up and run to beg at Abraham's feet. She might have made him angry or, pleading with him, she might have dissuaded him. But look what happened! But wait a minute... There is one more chance: Ishmael. He is just a small child. We have never met before. Let's see how much he can endure."

Azazel quickened his steps.

Realizing that Azazel had made new calculations, Yağmur and Servant barely were able to reach him by running. When Ishmael, who was walking behind Abraham, felt a shadow at his side, he suddenly turned around and saw that a man he had never seen before was following him. Without losing any time, Azazel immediately opened the topic and said:

"What a nice child you are. Where is your father taking you? On an outing?"

"No, I guess we are going to gather wood."

Shaking his head as if to say, "I don't think so," Azazel said:

"Look, my lovely child. I swear to the Lord of your father that he is taking you to a place where he will cut your throat shortly."

"Why would my father cut my throat?"

"Because his Lord commanded him to do so."

After these words which would shortly make him regret them, Azazel was crushed by the answer he received from the small child, Ishmael:

"In that case, whatever our Lord commanded, he definitely must do. God's command is respected by all of us."

In spite of this answer, Azazel persisted and he tried to fool Ishmael with lies one after another. He astonished Yağmur.

"Doesn't he ever give up?"

"Never," Servant replied. "He never gives up on a person until his last breath. I am not going to commend this effort, but I think that all Servants have to be at least this determined."

Distressed by this man's pressuring him, Ishmael was forced to complain to his father. When Abraham said, "Throw rocks at him," Ishmael did so with pleasure.

Even though Azazel kept his distance to avoid the rocks, he returned a little later. While he was still trying to make himself heard to Ishmael, the boy again began stoning him. Retreating, Azazel crouched in a corner after being stoned at his third attempt and he began to curiously follow what was happening. Yes, he was curious because there still might be something that didn't go well and he might have a new opportunity. Yağmur, comparing him to a hyena in this situation, rubbed his neck which was still hurting. When Servant said, "Let's go back," Yağmur was taken aback and asked:

"But why? Aren't we going to see what will happen?"

"You won't be able to endure what you will shortly see, Yağmur," responded Servant with compassion in his voice.

"I don't believe this. Is innocent blood going to flow?"

"Yes!"

"But how can this be? Isn't Ishmael one of God's Prophets? How can God allow such a thing?"

"Ah, Yağmur! You have such a pure heart. I have no doubt that in the future you will be a Servant just like your grandfather. Yes, it's true that blood will flow, but it won't be Ishmael's blood. The blood of a ram brought from the Holy Sphere by Gabriel will flow. But you cannot endure seeing Gabriel. That's what I meant to say. You can only see him when he is in the form of a human being. But still I will tell briefly what happened."

Hearing this, Yağmur felt better.

"When Abraham asked his son if he had any last desire, Ishmael listed them concisely:

'My dear father, tie my hands and feet securely so that I won't flounder too much and give trouble to you. Gather your clothing well so that blood doesn't splatter on it; otherwise, my mother will see it and feel sorrow. Strike with all your might so that my death comes easy. Put me face-down because perhaps you will be merciful when you see my face and you won't be able to fulfill the command.

Also don't let me see the knife because I might get scared. Also give my greetings to my mother.' After that Abraham struck the knife on Ishmael's throat with all of his might. But nothing happened. He tried again and still the knife didn't cut. When for the third time he struck the knife with all of his strength, but it still didn't cut, Abraham had no doubt that this was God's doing. Just at that moment saying, 'God is the Greatest, God is the Greatest,' Gabriel came with a ram in hand. Seeing him, Abraham replied with joy, 'God is the Greatest' and 'All praise be to God.' Wanting to express his thanks for what had happened, Ishmael also joined in saying, 'God is the Greatest and 'All praise be to God.''"

Then looking at Yağmur, who could not hold back his tears, Servant continued:

"Yes, successfully passing this test, Abraham, Hagar and Ishmael gave Azazel a great defeat. I am sure that if we don't count what happened today in the headquarters of the Army of Evil, what you saw has made you very happy."

"Absolutely! If I have to be honest, I was quite afraid. But how did they understand we were there?"

"Actually they weren't aware of me, but they felt your presence. However, if you hadn't closed your eyes as I warned you not to do, they could not have seen you either."

"Why just my presence? What did I do?"

"Look, Yağmur, I told you this game has rules, do you remember?"

"Yes!

"According to these rules, it is only possible for them to harm you with one condition: Your giving them permission. All the desires you keep in your heart are like entrance doors for them. Catching the smell of these desires there, Azazel felt your presence. If you were aware of it, he found you by smelling. Where do you think he found the things he offered you then? He repeated all the desires one-by-one that he was able to smell in you. It was going well except for one mistake he made: your grandfather. Yes, when he put forth your desire to be like your grandfather, he never thought you would carry such a desire in your heart. For whoever's heart he checks out, he finds nothing but worldly desires like those in your heart. If he had not made this mistake, we would have been in big trouble."

"You mean Azazel knew everything passing through my heart?"

"No, not exactly. He only acts with the information given to him by a spy in your heart."

"Who is this traitor?"

"It's your ego, Yağmur, your ego. The ego is the source of all those devilish desires."

"Will you get angry if I tell you that I'm a little confused?"

"No, absolutely not. Tomorrow we are going to such a place that you will see exactly what I mean in all its details. Only be prepared. This will be a special operation. It will take a long time. For this reason, I want you to come at the Morning Prayer."

"Operation? You mean like in the movies?

"I don't know what ridiculousness is happening in that black box, but this is going to be a full rescue operation. We are going to rescue a captive."

"I'm already excited. I'm going to wait impatiently for tomorrow."

"In that case, I entrust you to God. You know the exit!"

...

As Yağmur was returning home that evening, he gathered together in his mind what he had learned so far. Although human beings were not at fault, there was a war going on that Azazel had started on his own. Consequently, it was necessary for every human being to fight against Azazel and his army in order to protect himself. However, very few people could see the situation like this. The remaining majority were absolutely unaware that the devil was their biggest enemy and that if they were defeated, they would share the same fate as the devil.

The Prophets and the Divine Books were all sent for the purpose of warning mankind. All monotheistic religions had explained that the devil was a clear enemy, what means he used to defeat people, and what precautions must be taken in order to oppose him and be saved. However, this duty being abandoned now at a time when there were no Prophets was like spreading butter on Azazel's bread. Someone had to spoil his game and, bravely taking a stance before the Army of Evil, should take all impartial people behind them. But in the absence of the Prophets, who could perform this duty? With the exception of Azazel and his army, Yağmur was now one of those who knew best the answer to this question: The Servants! Yes, with their minds, goods, lives, positions and time—with all their beings—these volunteer soldiers had sworn to give their all against this evil power and to never give up throughout this struggle.

Yağmur had seen with his own eyes a few of these encounters that sometimes resulted in victory and sometimes in defeat. He had gained some knowledge of Azazel's offensive tactics and had met some extraordinary people who had repelled these attacks. However, he was thinking that for himself and ordinary people like himself, this was not enough on the subject of defeating the devil and that there were many more things he had to learn. Especially about the "Ego."

According to what Servant said, until this traitor inside of us who spied for the devil was taken under control, it was not possible to talk about victory in this struggle. The "operation" he mentioned must be related to this. Perhaps a person could fight with an enemy standing opposite to him, but it was much more difficult to struggle with a spy who had infiltrated one's own line. Suddenly feeling helpless, he said, "As if the devil is a small problem, now the ego is also in this work!" But there was something that he did not yet know: If it weren't for the ego, man would be no different from the angels and there would be no need to create human beings. In this case, the ego was nothing other than a poor creature that spoke the same language as the devil and that desired things that God forbade as a test.

When he entered the house, he smelled the dinner that was ready. After sticking his head in the kitchen doorway and saying hello, he changed his clothes and sat down at the dinner table. Bothered by his silent and contemplative situation throughout dinner, Rehnüma said:

"I'm very bored. Shall we watch television after dinner? There's a really good movie today."

Yağmur no longer thought very positively about television which Servant had called "a black box full of nonsense." But when he realized that he had neglected Rehnüma a lot recently, he could not refuse this small request.

The film was just the kind that Yağmur liked. A secret service agent who had infiltrated the mafia was giving information to headquarters regarding crimes that would take place and he was trying to capture the head of the gang. Of course, when several jobs went wrong, it was immediately understood that there was a spy in the gang. The means the head of the gang chose to uncover the spy was a very classic, but effective method.

He gave the suspected man several orders that he would not like. One of them was the worst. The agent was to get into a gun fight with his police friends. This was truly a difficult situation for him. Well, what did he do? He shot two of his friends! Even if the bullets just grazed them, he did it. Not only did this remove suspicion from him, but it enabled him to become the gang leader's top man. Of course, what followed is obvious!

Even while Yağmur was watching these, he was going to different realms. He had a very interesting idea. He realized that Azazel was a spy among the angels and that his trickery became apparent with God's command to "bow to Adam." Always commanding things that pleased Azazel until that time, God commanded him to do something he didn't want to do for the first time. As a result, the spy became obvious. In this case, a person could flush out the spy hiding in his inner world by the same means.

When he thought of these things, Yağmur got so excited. This means that when the inner spy is confronted with something it doesn't want to do, he immediately shows himself. He immediately tried to find several examples to prove his thesis.

A simple example immediately came to mind. It had just occurred last week. When he came home in the evening, Rehnüma said before dinner, "I did the cleaning today and I'm a little tired. If it's not to much trouble, can you hang these curtains? We have to hang them before they dry so they don't get wrinkled!" It was as if she had said, "You don't do anything all day long. You just sit at your desk all day long. The least you can do is hang these curtains!" He suddenly became so angry that he replied to these words that actually had never been uttered by Rehnüma: "And what have you done all day long? Did you wait for me to hang the curtains? If you're not going to clean the house, then what are you going to do?"

Now he thought this way about that event. What was he really angry about? He couldn't have been mad about his wife's words because she had spoken very courteously and innocently. He could not have become angry about what she wanted because it was an extremely simple request that he could easily do and that he had more than enough strength to do. In this case, there could only be one reason for the response he gave: Someone inside of him didn't want to do it. He wanted the table to be set immediately and to fill his stomach. But hanging the curtains was not among his desires, especially being forced to do something he didn't want to do! At the expense of uncovering himself, he had opposed this. Yes, the agent was uncovered.

It was his last year in middle school. There was no lesson because the turism teacher hadn't come. It was chaos. When the noise grew so loud that it echoed in all the corridors, the teacher on hall duty suddenly opened the door and gave a sharp warning to the whole class. In other words, everyone had been asked to quiet down including himself. But for some reason, he didn't want to be quiet. Although it had been forbidden to talk, someone inside of him was opposing this prohibition. In fact, he not only talked, but he stood on the top of his desk and shouted. Of course, this situation was only able to continue until the teacher on duty suddenly came into the classroom.

Of course, he would not have knocked on the door before entering. If the teacher had done that, he would have jumped down but at that moment the situation was like this: One hand was waving his tie in the air and the other hand was on his waist like the leader of a folk dance. The two buttons on his shirt had popped off and he was sweating all over. When the teacher entered the room, it was as if he didn't see the other noise-makers but looked directly at him. You can imagine what followed. He would never forget the single slap he received for the first time in his life from a teacher. There was a prohibition and there was "someone inside" who didn't want to obey. However, the pain of the slap he received was felt by his whole body and not just the "one inside."

"So the balance between God and His servant is something like this!" he said. "God puts some rules, and then because of a traitor who doesn't want to obey these, I am punished, too. It's understood. What needs to be done is to get rid of this secret agent."

"Servant will love this idea."

"Did you say something to me?"

As Yağmur was saying, "No dear, I'm talking to myself," he became aware of the titles written on the black background. But actually the real film was just beginning...

# Rescue Operation

It was Sunday and when he approached the cemetery for the Morning Prayer, Yağmur realized that there was no light inside. Even worse, the entrance gate to the cemetery was locked. While joking, "It's obvious that the cemetery and the mosque in it are closed for the Morning Prayer. The angels of death can't be on official holiday," he was actually trying to suppress the fear inside of him. This was characteristic of his that Yağmur didn't like. But whenever he became up tight, he tried to find something funny about the situation he was in to relax himself. He had gotten a lot of headaches from doing this.

As he was about to park his car in front of the gate, he remembered that today's work could last a long time so he pulled his car over to the side. Realizing that he was not going to be able to jump over the high iron bars of the entrance gate which was locked at this hour in the morning, he turned towards one of the walls. Jumping over the wall with difficulty, Yağmur said, "Servant is right. This fully resembles an operation." Then he added laughing, "Rescue Operation! I wonder which dead person we are going to rescue."

He was thinking that he had never been this much afraid when he remembered what had happened in Azazel's headquarters. The worst part was that now he had begun to be even more afraid. What if Azazel would suddenly appear before him in this dark cemetery? What if one of the dead got up from its grave and caught him by the foot? What if a werewolf jumped out from behind that tree? While, on the one hand, these thoughts came to his mind, on the other hand, the films he watched were bothering him. He said to himself, "I shouldn't have watched those terrible films!"

Yağmur finally reached the mosque, but the door was locked. He went to the courtyard, which was the only place he could perform his Prayers, and spread his coat on the slab where coffins are placed. He performed the shortest Prayer of his life because "it was better than not praying at all."

While he ran towards the grave, he couldn't help but grumble to Servant. He hadn't reached it yet, but he had already begun to recite the chapter Al-Fatiha. Indifferent even to the pain of his leg which he had hit on the corner of the grave because his eyes were closed, he said "Amen!" and opened his eyes.

The first thing he wanted to do as soon as he opened his eyes was to criticize Servant, but what he saw made him suddenly forget all about those moments of fear. He could only say:

"Just like in dreams."

"It is, isn't it?" Servant affirmed. Yağmur's curiosity was blatant enough to obstruct the pleasure of watching the scenery:

"Where is this?"

"This is the City of the Heart, the capitol of the Country of Body. The whole country is ruled by the palace you see in the middle."

Yağmur could only say enchantedly:

"It's beautiful."

"If we do not succeed in the operation that I mentioned to you, none of this beauty will remain."

"What do you mean?"

"Come here! We have to hurry. I'll explain to you along the way."

They began to descend from the green hill they were standing on. Everyplace was full of fruit trees, each one more beautiful than the next. The streams coming from five different directions each turned into a waterfall as it emptied into the lake just behind the palace. The water particles rising at that moment brought about a magnificent rainbow. Also, there were five different gates in the walls surrounding the palace and people were constantly entering and leaving the city through these. There were separate roads opening from each gate and they were all full of caravans. Yağmur couldn't even see in front of himself due to his looking at the beauty around him. It was amazing, but he didn't ask any questions. Finally Servant broke the silence:

"What happened, Yağmur? I guess you couldn't find any thing to ask about."

"I don't know. Everything appears to be OK. This country must have a very good sultan."

"This may sound strange, but did you know that this country doesn't have a sultan?"

"Then why doesn't this order break down? Who rules this country?"

"The grand vizier. Don't ever forget this! Countries are ruled by viziers and not sultans. Viziers are ruled by sultans!"

"OK. As a result, isn't it the sultan who rules?"

"But I told you that this country doesn't have a sultan."

"Then I would say that the vizier is doing a very good job."

"Don't be fooled by appearances! Look around carefully."

At that moment they had drawn very close to the city. They had entered closely enough to hear the voices of the people around them. Servant said:

"Come and let's talk with these people a little. Maybe you will understand the situation better."

They went up to four or five people sitting at the side who were drinking and gambling. Servant started off the conversation:

"Hello, guys. You seem to be having a good time."

"That's right, man," one of them replied.

Servant asked: "What are you doing here?"

"We're drinking and having fun. Sit down and let's hang out together. Alcohol is free in this country. Don't worry, we're not going to take money from you. Thanks to 'Sir Ego.'"

"What work do you do?" Yağmur asked.

They all broke out into laughter. One of them tried to answer as well as he could:

"Work? You talk about working. That's not a problem for us. Just like alcohol and gambling, thievery is also free in this country. Everyone's goods are shared by everyone ... thanks to our vizier!"

Yağmur had grown uncomfortable so Servant said: "Let's go."

They continued to walk. While Yağmur realized how wrong he had been, he was angry both with himself and the vizier whom he had not yet met. He said angrily:

"You said a "Rescue Operation." I hope you meant to kill the vizier and save the country."

"No," replied Servant smiling. "It's not that easy. The situation is a little confusing. As I said, viziers rule the country. These people never met their sultan. The power of the current vizier, Sir Ego, increased so much during the previous four-month long interval between succession that removing him would drag the whole country into great chaos. You saw how he increased his power. Making everything the people wanted free, he gained their love so much that they will not recognize any other ruler. However, it is also true that if he continues to rule like this, chaos and anarchy await this country for sure. It's our duty to rescue the country from this probable chaos. Of course, you too have understood that this is not going to be done by killing the vizier."

"What are we going to do then?"

The thing that needs to be done in a rescue operation: We're going to save the sultan."

"Is the sultan alive?"

"Yes, according to our intelligence information, he is being held in a prison far from the palace. If we don't hurry, we might lose him. We must be invisible throughout this operation. Especially in the palace. For this reason, I want you to read this verse from the chapter Ya-Sin: '*Wa ja'alna min bayni aydihim saddan wa min khalfihim saddan fa aghshaynahum fahum la yubsirun* (We have surrounded them with such a wall both in front of them and behind them that even if they look, they cannot see). In order to become visible again, read these two verses from the chapter Al-Balad: '*Ayahsabu an lam yarahu ahad. Alam naj'alahu aynayn.*' (Does he think no one saw him? Didn't we give him two eyes?) Take this paper. Thinking that you don't know them, I wrote the verses here."

"Thank you very much. You are very kind, but since it's dangerous, why do we need to be visible?"

"Putting everything else aside, Sultan 'Master Spirit' must see us. At any rate, later on you will not be able to be invisible again. But adjust your timing very well. Because everyplace will be full of Grand Vizier Ego's spies."

"OK, when do we start?"

"Immediately, now!"

## Vacant Throne

The main entrance to the palace was quite magnificent. On the door the words *La ilaha illallah. Muhammadu'r-Rasulullah* (There is no deity but God. Muhammad is His Messenger) were written in gold letters, and there was a curious note just underneath:

"The entrance to this door is from within!"

Regardless of how much he thought about it, Yağmur could not understand the wisdom of these words.

Now what did this mean? The door was for entering, but the entrance to the door was from within. The more he thought, the more confused Yağmur became. "Sometimes it's best not to think, but to believe," he said. Regarding the workers who had climbed a ladder, he thought, "I guess they're polishing the gold letters."

The long corridors resembled a labyrinth. Although they heard vague speech echoing from every side, nothing could be understood because all the voices became mixed up with one another. They started following a group of soldiers, one of whom was obviously a commander. Apparently they had some important work to do. First right, then left, then left again, then. These corridors were so confusing that it was impossible for them to find anyplace on their own. For this reason, they stayed with the soldiers and after a long and zigzagging walk, they finally stopped.

In front of a large door the man dressed like a commander said to the officials:

"Inform the Grand Vizier that I'm here."

Their guess was correct. The official opened the door and shouted inside:

"Commander Anger has come!"

They went in all together. It was a rather large hall. There was alcohol, gambling tables and miserable slaves everywhere. But something even stranger, more pitiable and sadder than these caught Yağmur's attention: An empty throne. It was set up in the best place in the hall, but it was a vacant throne. Commander Anger began to speak... Or more accurately, he began to roar:

"I see that the workers at the entrance are still working."

"Those despicable men. They weren't able to remove the writing," said the Grand Vizier with a rasping voice.

Yağmur understood from this that the gold letters were not being polished.

Commander Anger continued roaring:

"Is the treasury so poor that we only have that gold left?"

"I didn't give the command for that writing to be removed only for the treasury; I ordered it because of the writing under the gold," Grand Vizier Ego said. He was talking about the writing that Yağmur had not been able to understand.

Yağmur continued listening to the Grand Vizier with increased curiosity. It said, "The entrance to this door is from within." In other words, there was no permission from entering from outside. If we remove the writing on the top, then everyone who wants to can enter the palace. It was obvious that the commander's question, "But why should we want this?" made the Grand Vizier apprehensive:

"You stay out of that matter. Tell me about our plans to attack our neighboring country."

Before the commander had a chance to answer, someone entered in a rage. Walking quickly towards the Grand Vizier, this person must have been important because the soldiers all made way for him.

"I heard that you ordered the writing on the entrance to be removed. You know that together with that writing being the country's ideograph, it is our only defense against our sworn enemies. I cannot permit such a thing."

"Calm down, Sir Conscience. You know that you, not I, are the second vizier here. I swear I had no other thought but for it to be a contribution to the treasury. Also, it hasn't been removed yet. Don't make such hasty sallies, OK?"

"I don't think that Sir Conscience is being unfair," said someone whom Yağmur had not distinguished from the slaves.

He continued:

"You call his action hasty, but what good will it do to protest after the writing is removed?"

The Grand Vizier got a little upset with this man appearing as a slave:

"Oh, Sir Intelligence, are you here? You must have finished the work I gave you in order to be able to think such empty thoughts. It would be better if you immediately follow Commander Anger and think about the plans for attack. I don't want to be made a fool of this time. Our last defeat cost us dearly. If you have time after my work, you can help Sir Conscience."

Sir Conscience gave a sharp criticism:

"Ah, Sir Intelligence! You are the third vizier in the palace with authority. What does the Grand Vizier give you that you act as his slave? How much I would like for you to help me in the absence of our sultan!"

Sir Conscience had such a pleasant voice that it went directly to the heart of those listening and turned all the stones there upside-down. These words were just about to affect Sir Intelligence when the Grand Vizier immediately started shouting to prevent this and to close the subject:

"What do you mean by that? Sir Intelligence is only helping me in my work. When he becomes tired from working so hard, he relaxes here with this revelry, that's all. You don't need to blow this out of proportions. OK, everyone back to their own job."

Servant immediately pulled Yağmur aside and mentioned his plan:

"Look Yağmur, the situation is worse than we thought. If that writing on the entrance door is removed, Azazel and his army can immediately come and this throne you see will not remain vacant. That is just what the Grand Vizier has been trying to do: putting Azazel on the throne. If he can do this, neither Sir Conscience, who gives him a headache, nor imprisoned Master Spirit can remain here. The first thing they will do is to exile them. If we can save the sultan, things will change. The palace administration still knows him and will listen to him."

Servant added:

"Now we need to separate. I am going to talk with Sir Conscience. I have to help him so that the writing on the door won't be removed. Meanwhile, you try and learn where Master Spirit is being held captive. Let's meet here again at sunset. We'll plan what to do at that time."

When Servant left after Sir Conscience, Yağmur remained alone in the large hall. He took a few sips from the glass Sir Ego's slaves gave him. When it was said, "Come on! Let the entertainment continue," various kinds of debauchery began. Feeling very uncomfortable, Yağmur immediately left.

In order to be able to return here again at sunset, he took out a piece of paper and a pen from his pocket. He thought that a drawing he would make as he proceeded would make his job easier. While going through corridors whose destinations were unknown, it occurred to him that there had been no documents in the large hall. "There must be an office where the Grand Vizier's documents are kept. Maybe I can find a clue there," he thought. But it was certain that finding this office was not going to be easy. There were many rooms on each corridor, but nothing was written on any of them. He turned his ear to the servants walking around. Maybe he could hear something about the Grand Vizier's office. The conversation between two servants who passed him with buckets, mops and cleaning cloths on their carts was very helpful:

"Where are you going to clean today?"

"I'm going to clean their bedrooms. And you?"

"Your job is easy. I'm going to the administration floor. So it's going to be a long day."

"Now I really feel sorry for you. No, if it weren't for that long, boring procedure at the door of every room, it wouldn't be so bad. Especially recently they have really increased security measures."

Saying, "I guess they think we are coming to make assassination, not cleaning," both men began to laugh. Finding out what he had wanted to know, Yağmur followed the cleaning man who said he was going to the administration floor.

This was the top floor of the palace and the whole corridor was full of rooms to the right and left. He had to be very careful, because there was a soldier at every door and even though Yağmur was invisible, he knew well that he shouldn't touch anything. He did the most logical thing that came to mind. While the servant talked with the soldier at the door and explained how bothered he was by being searched, Yağmur quietly sat on the edge of the cart the worker had left at the side. When the door opened and the cleaner began to push the cart, he began to complain about how hard it was to push the cart:

"O my God! Will evening ever come today?"

As soon as he entered the room, the cleaner quickly closed the door and headed towards the desk. Yağmur was surprised because the room was sparkling clean and the cleaner didn't seem to be going to clean it. With the key in his hand, he opened the drawer under the desk and took out some papers. Then he put the paper he took out of his pocket and, placing it on top of the others, he put them back into the drawer. He had just extended his hand to lock the drawer, when Yağmur thought he had to do something fast. If the drawer would be locked, it would not be possible for him to open it again. He did the first thing that came to his mind: He turned over the bucket full of water and stood aside. Startled by the bucket overturning in the middle of the room, the cleaner, complaining loudly, immediately went to get the mop from the cart and Yağmur went behind the desk. Without looking to see what it was about, he quietly took one of the papers and put it in his pocket. The cleaner mopped the spilled water and came towards Yağmur to lock the drawer. This time Yağmur passed under the desk and again sat down on the front of the cleaning cart. When the worker knocked on the door to get out, the soldier opened the locked door and said:

"Your work finished quickly; you're fast today."

The cleaner replied:

"There wasn't much to do today. It's cleaned everyday. Also, our Grand Vizier is a very clean person." Then he pushed the cart out the door, not understanding why it was so difficult to push the cart today.

Yağmur silently got off the cart when it stopped in front of the next door and tip-toed back in the direction he had come. Finding a place where he could be alone, he wanted to see what was written on the paper. His curiosity made him hurry even more so that he quietly entered the first open room on the floor below. When he was sure no one else was there, he slowly closed the door. Although the paper he took from his pocket was not a roadmap to the prison, it was at least as important as that...

## Secret Alliance

The following was written on the paper:

"From the rebel Azazel who was cursed by God,

An anxiety to my dear friend and future vizier Sir Ego: According to the gathered intelligence, your removing the writing from the entrance door to the palace will enable us to achieve our work without any interference.

I estimate that Sir Conscience will oppose you on this subject. Deal with him lightly as he wishes. Divert him with things he wants to hear and be yourself; do not allow him to join with Sir Intelligence. What you need to do for this is to keep Sir Intelligence busy with unnecessary things and to divert him with a lot of entertainment in his spare time.

Finally, highly increase security precautions at the palace! We have heard that a covert operation is going to be made by several men who have been given special assignment from the Servants' Unit of the Army of Good. You know well that these Servants are very dangerous men. They won't give up until they have accomplished their job. You will remember what difficulties we had with them in the past. If this is an operation for the sultan, know that it can ruin our efforts.

May God's trouble and damnation be upon you!

Commander-in-Chief of the Army of Evil, Azazel"

Yağmur understood everything much better now. Saying to himself, "So things work like this here, Sir Ego! You lowly traitor!" he felt that his inner hatred had increased even more. He thought about what an important job Servant was doing by helping Sir Conscience to prevent the writing from being removed from the door. Meanwhile, as he leaned his head out the window and realized that it was about to be dark, he immediately headed towards the large hall.

He was thinking about the latest anxiety letter that had come today from Azazel. He thought that if he could read these letters which came regularly everyday, he could take precautions before things that were to happen. Once the letters entered the room, reading them would be very difficult. It occurred to him that if he followed the letter-carrying informant who was disguised as a cleaner, he might find an opportunity to read the letter before it was taken to the room. However, he would have to put it back after he read it, because if the Grand Vizier, who was already informed on these matters, didn't see the letter, everything would become apparent and the whole operation could collapse. The letter in his pocket must be one of the older ones so Yağmur was comfortable that its absence would be more difficult to discern.

In order to enter the hall, he stood in front of it and waited for someone to come and enter. His timing was so good that a little later he saw Sir Conscience and Servant at the end of the corridor. They went through the door opened for Sir Conscience one after another.

At that moment someone resembling a messenger was giving information to the Grand Vizier:

"Sir, also we received news of a caravan full of food in a place near the "Mouth Road." According to the scouts, most of the camels are loaded with fresh fruit; the rest carry honey and olives."

"Great! Immediately forward my command to the commander of the second army, "Commander Lust." He should catch the caravan with his men without losing any time. He should confiscate the goods and bring those from the caravan here as captives."

As the messenger who said "At your command, sir," was leaving the room, Sir Conscience walked towards the Grand Vizier and, without hesitating to speak the truth, said:

"What kind of job is this, Sir Ego? We are a state, not a group of bandits! If we need some food for our treasury, there are more appropriate ways like working and earning it. Isn't that so, Sir Intelligence? Why don't you say something, too?"

Complaining that he was busy, Sir Intelligence answered:

"I'm busy right now with a very important matter that Sir Ego wanted me to think about. As you know, I can't think of two things at the same time."

Exactly in conformance with the advice Azazel gave in the letter in Yağmur's hand, Sir Ego found a way to silence Sir Conscience:

"Look Sir Conscience! I believe you are absolutely right. Just let the caravan goods come and then we'll decide what to do. You can be certain that I will take your ideas into consideration. Please trust me."

Yağmur said to himself:

"Trust you? Who can trust you, lowly traitor? Soon all your tricks will be revealed."

Then, calling Servant to a corner of the hall, he wanted to share what they had learned:

"Every day one of their servants regularly puts a letter from Azazel in the study of the Grand Vizier. All directions reach him in this way. If we find a way to see what is written in those letters, we can take precautions accordingly; what do say?"

"Very good Yağmur! This is very valuable information. Try and learn what he wrote in tomorrow's letter. Together with Sir Conscience, I am going to continue to try and prevent the entrance writing from being removed from the door. Today we kept the workers busy with unbelievable things. However, this cannot last long. We have to immediately find the prison where Master Spirit is being held."

Servant realized that things had gotten out of hand again. The viziers were arguing with one another again. The cause of this was what a messenger had said:

"Sir, as you previously ordered, our spies are monitoring our neighboring country's beautiful princess, 'Sultan Stranger.' According to news that just came, the beautiful princess has passed to a neighboring country using the "Eye Road." Other than ten guards, there is no one with her, sir. What is your command?"

The diabolical look in Sir Ego's eyes had never been this disgusting. He immediately commanded:

"Great! This is the long-awaited opportunity. I told her, 'I'll trap you in an isolated place.' Send a messenger to Commander Lust urgently. As soon as he finishes his work on the Mouth Road, he should pass to the Eye Road without losing time. He shouldn't come until he has gotten Sultan Stranger!"

"As you command, sir!"

Sir Conscience was in despair:

"Are you aware of what you have done, Sir Ego? How can a state official use his power like this for oppression? You should know that because of what you have done, we will all be in trouble!"

"Sir, I have no bad intentions! How can Princess Stranger go on this many roads without protection? Look it's also dark out now. We'll host her in our palace tonight and send her tomorrow with a division of soldiers. Is that so bad?"

While expressing his amazement to Servant saying, "This Grand Vizier is very dangerous and very clever," he received an even more astounding answer:

"Not at all actually," Servant said. "Sir Ego is a stupid idiot! But he gets all his intelligence from an extremely smart and that much despicable creature: Azazel. Sir Ego's only special quality is his unbelievable insistence on one subject. Like a child, he will do anything until he gets what he wants. Azazel is different from him. The minute he understands that one way hasn't worked for him, he immediately finds another way. You saw this with your own eyes in the situation with Abraham and his family. For this reason, it's very important to learn what he will write in his future letters. Sir Conscience mentioned the bedrooms on the upper floors. Most of them are empty. Now he is going to take us there. Rest well tonight; we have to start working early tomorrow morning."

Together with Sir Conscience, they went to the floor where the bedrooms were. These rooms had been planned for rest and relaxation for guests. Apparently there were no other guests but them in the palace. For now...

After Yağmur entered a room in the middle of the corridor that wouldn't attract attention, the others left. The room had a view of the lake behind the palace. It could be said to be the most beautiful room Yağmur had ever seen in his life. After enjoying the view a little, he understood how tired he was as soon as he put his head on the bird-feather pillow.

Not a half an hour had passed when he sprung from his bed at the sound of a scream. He opened the door slightly and looked down the corridor. The girl who the soldiers were pulling from her arm and who resembled a princess must be Sultan Stranger. They forced her into one of the rooms and locked the door.

Suddenly Yağmur's heroism surfaced again. It didn't take him long to decide:

"I have to save the princess somehow."

The soldiers had left the key on the door. Saying, "This is a great opportunity," he flew out of the room. But just as he approached the door, a rasping voice was heard from the stairs:

After saying, "Well done! Now tell everyone that I don't want anyone on this floor. We have to show our hospitality to the princess," his laughter resembling that of Azazel resounded throughout the whole corridor. It was none other than Sir Ego! Yağmur immediately drew to the side and began to think of another way to save the princess.

Meanwhile, the princess's screams for help were heard as soon as Sir Ego entered the room. Yağmur did the first thing that came to his mind as usual: He immediately pounded on the door and then retreated. The sounds inside immediately ceased. Even if temporarily, it had helped. Sir Ego furiously appeared at the door, but when he didn't see anyone at either end of the corridor, he went back inside. The princess has just started to shout again when Yağmur pounded on the door again. Sir Ego again came out, but when he didn't see anyone, he immediately locked the door and shouting at the servants, he turned towards the stairway leading to the lower floor. This was just the right moment. Yağmur immediately recited the two verses in the chapter Al-Balad and turned towards the room where the princess was. When he met with the screams of the princess as soon as the door opened, he hurriedly went to her side and said:

"Please be quiet, Princess! I have no intention of harming you. To the contrary, I want to rescue you from here." The princess calmed down a little and she wanted to learn how her rescuer was going to do this:

"Thank you very much! What is your plan? How are you going to rescue me?"

Not yet knowing the answer to this question, Yağmur wanted a little more time to think. If the princess tried to kill Sir Ego when he came after her or at least to wound him, she definitely would be thrown into prison. Maybe by this means Master Spirit could be reached. While searching his pockets with the hope of finding something to use for this, the letter Azazel had written to Sir Ego came to his hand. It was impossible to wound anyone with this, but maybe it could be used to fool someone. Especially an idiot like Sir Ego:

"Look Princess! We don't have much time. So listen carefully to what I'm going to say and please do exactly as I say. Take this letter. When Sir Ego comes here, I want you to immediately harshly oppose him. Say this: 'Look Sir Ego! You are not yet aware of who you are dealing with. I am Azazel's messenger. I have a secret letter he sent to Master Spirit. I absolutely have to get it to him. Or else you, too, can imagine what will happen.' Keep the letter folded in your hand like this. Extend it to Sir Ego so that he can only see the words, 'Commander-in-Chief of the Army of Evil, Azazel.' As soon as he sees it, pull the letter back and put it in your pocket. I think he'll come now. Even if you can't see me, I'll always be at your side. Please don't be afraid," he said and left the room quickly.

He had not yet read the verse in the chapter Ya-Sin when Sir Ego came with two soldiers at his side. He put them on watch at the head of the stairs and quickly entered the room.

A little later, curious about what had happened, Yağmur put his ear to the door and began to carefully listen to what was being said. A rasping voice was coming:

"Why didn't you tell me this from the beginning. It's a little strange for him to send a letter to the sultan, but our master Azazel knows best. Can I look and see what he wrote?"

"Don't even think of it. You know very well what our master Azazel does when he gets angry. For this reason, take me to the sultan as fast as possible."

"That boring guy called Sultan Spirit is in a special prison in the 'Cave of Heedlessness.' He is being punished for putting his nose into my work for years. It is about a half a day's distance from the palace. Tomorrow morning you can set out with two of my trusted men, Sleep and Comfort. No one else but them can take you to the Cave of Heedlessness."

"Can't we leave immediately?"

"You should be able to understand from their names! Both are dead asleep now. They usually don't get up before noon, but I'll wake them up early tomorrow morning for you. You rest, too. If you need anything... You know what I mean..."

"Get out of here! Don't press your luck!"

"Immediately, ma'am. Forgive me," Sir Ego said. But even as he was leaving the room he couldn't help but look slyly at the princess.

Yağmur went to the room and thanked the princess as soon as the Grand Vizier left.

The princess replied:

"Actually I must thank you. You saved me from the hands of this vile one. Although I was doubtful as to whether this idea was going to be helpful, everything went well."

Yağmur continued talking:

"Everything went well with your help. You really performed your role well. Now it's a good idea to rest. I think you have had a hard day. Before I forget, I will be pleased if you continue this pretence tomorrow. I have no other way to reach the sultan. I can only go there through you. Don't worry. Even though you can't see me, I'll be with you tomorrow."

"What does that mean? You said the same thing a little earlier. How can I not see someone at my side?"

"It's a little difficult to explain this, but please trust me! If you help me rescue the sultan, I will explain everything to you. Now I have to go. Good night."

# The Secret in the Cave of Heedlessness

Yağmur spent the whole night in front of the room where Sultan Stranger was staying. He wanted to be sure that no harm came to her and he was afraid of missing the journey tomorrow morning. He was startled by the voices of a group of soldiers that came together with the first rays of the sun and he began to wait in a corner. A long period of following began with the princess leaving her room.

Two horsemen and a carriage were waiting in front of the palace. If you look at the fact that the two horsemen were yawning, then they must be Sleep and Comfort. It was obvious in every way that they were not happy with their situation. While the princess proceeded towards the carriage, she looked all around. Yağmur understood that she was looking for him. Acting a little faster than her, he took his place at the back of the carriage and a half day discomforting journey began.

Just as they were leaving the main city gate, he saw Sir Ego in a corner with his servant from a few days before. After their conversation, the servant got on his horse, passed through the gate and swiftly rode away.

Obviously Sir Ego was sending news to Azazel in this way. The feeling inside Yağmur that soon some very bad things would happen began to surface. He understood that the sultan had to be rescued today or all this effort would be for naught.

However, suddenly something came to mind. Why was he going to rescue the sultan? As far as he could see, the people were very happy with their situation. Until now he hadn't run into anyone except for Sir Conscience who was complaining about the situation. He thought, "I wonder how Servant would answer this question?" I guess he would say that before anything else this operation was a command. Actually that's true. It was a command. A command given to us from the Holy Sphere. So the sultan's rescue was very important both for him and the people.

"Of course! If we don't rescue the sultan, Azazel will come and sit on that throne. Maybe he is promising things that are pleasing to everyone now, but what was said to him as he was being driven from God's presence explains this very well: 'What can Satan promise except deceit?' Yes, absolutely! He will deceive everyone including Sir Ego with these promises and make them partner to his perverse fortune. Because he permitted it, Master Spirit would get his share from this pitiful end." With these thoughts, Yağmur had found his answers.

A long time had passed since their journey began, but Yağmur had not heard the speech of these two valuable men of Sir Ego. He looked ahead to see what was happening. He couldn't believe his eyes. These two men called Sleep and Comfort were sleeping on horseback. The carriage driver must have been suspicious because he called out to these two wretches:

"Gentlemen! Are you sleeping? Where are we going like this?"

His shouts aroused the one whose sleep was lighter. He became startled and responded:

"To the Cave of Heedlessness of course."

"Fine, but how will we go there when you're not looking around, but you're just snoring?"

"That's the secret of the Cave of Heedlessness. People who are awake like you can never find its place. The only way to find it is to become heedless. Just like the sultan did before he was imprisoned there. Don't worry, heedlessness will show us the way. If you bother me again, we won't even be able to find it by evening. So be quiet now," he said and lowering his head, he continued what he was doing.

Sighing, Yağmur said:

"So the sultan is just like me! I also like sleeping a lot. Although since I met Servant I haven't had a really good night's sleep. But anyhow!"

The long, uncomfortable and boring journey ended at the skirts of a huge mountain. As soon as the princess got down from the carriage, Sleep and Comfort began to proceed with her. Thinking that this situation would make it more difficult to rescue the sultan, the princess protested:

"No, not like this. I have to see Master Spirit alone. You stay here!"

"But what will happen to the food we have brought for the sultan? We always meet his daily needs."

"Then I will go first. My business won't take much time. Then you can meet his needs. Plus, it's been a long trip. You will have rested here a little."

"OK then, why didn't you say so?"

They were obviously pleased with the idea of sleeping.

Thinking, "This princess is a lot smarter than she appears," Yağmur began to follow her. The entrance to the cave was near the peak of the mountain. Saying, "The poor sultan! Who knows what difficulties he experienced here," he formed a picture of a prison in his mind.

After the large iron fence the place was at most four square meters, damp, dim, smelly and cold. When they arrived at the mouth of the cave, Yağmur waited a little for the princess to proceed. It was interesting that there was no soldier in sight. While thinking, "They have locked the door from the outside and abandoned the poor guy," the sound of the princess's echoing voice was heard:

"Honorable Sultan! Honorable Sultan!"

Thinking that everything was OK, Yağmur recited the two verses in the chapter Al-Balad and entered. According to what Servant had said, he would see the sultan and there would be no need for him to become invisible again. He noticed the prison's iron fence near the entrance to the cave. The princess was calling out just in front of the fence and there was some 3 or 4 day-old food there that had flies on it. When the princess heard his footsteps, she turned back.

"You? How did you come here? I constantly watched for you, but I never saw you."

Saying, "This situation is a little confusing, princess; I'll explain later," he reached the prison. The inside was not at all like he thought. There was everything for a person's ease and comfort. Yağmur curiously shouted inside:

"Honorable Sultan! Dear Master Spirit! My God, how strange this is. I hope this is not a trick of Sir Ego. No, he's too stupid to think of this. Plus, the two riders who brought us here were sure the Sultan is here. Since they come everyday and bring what he needs... Although I don't understand why this food is still here. Also the prison's door is still locked. It would be very difficult to escape from here. If he were hiding, he should come when he heard our voices. At any rate, there's one thing I know and that is that the Sultan is not here."

Yağmur seemed to be talking to himself instead of to the princess until she interrupted:

"Then let me hear your story. You keep saying that you will explain later. Don't forget that I'm a princess and I expect you to keep your word to me."

Yağmur began to explain. They were walking downhill. He explained in detail how he had come to this country, what his real purpose was, Servant, and what he had lived in the last twenty-four hours. He was comfortably explaining these because it didn't even occur to him that the princess might believe him. The princess was listening enchantedly as if she were hearing a story—until she was startled by the voices of two men shouting:

"Honorable Sultan! This is Honorable Sultan!"

Yağmur and the princess began to look around. Honorable Sultan was here some place. It was necessary to immediately protect him. However, the two shouting men, Sleep and Comfort, were pointing to Yağmur. Hesitating for a moment, Yağmur quickly turned around, but he didn't see anything.

Either these two who did nothing but sleep day and night were still in a dream world or... There was no "or!" What else could it be? But their amazement was perfectly obvious. Their eyes were so wide-open that probably no one had ever seen their sleepy eyes like this. They were approaching Yağmur.

They were walking towards him with questions like, "Sir, how did you get out of prison? Why haven't you taken the food for several days?"

He immediately read the verse in the chapter Ya-Sin, but he realized that it hadn't helped when he saw that no one was surprised. When as a last resort, he was about to run away, he understood that these two would not harm him when they kissed the skirts of his robe. They didn't know how to give him enough respect. In addition to

Yağmur, the princess was also amazed by this situation. Her astonishment was not from Yağmur's not being able to be the sultan, but from what he had just explained being able to be a lie.

The return trip should have been much more comfortable for Yağmur, but it wasn't at all. While coming, there was just one question in his mind: "How can I save the Sultan?" But now, beginning with "What's going on?" there were hundreds of questions to be answered that returned to the beginning with "If I am the sultan." And he knew very well who he was going to get these answers from. While impatient to return immediately to the palace, he said:

"If we could go a little faster..."

The princess simultaneously stuck her head out the window and said:

"Didn't you hear the Sultan? He wants you to go faster."

Yağmur got the answer to some of those questions at that moment. They suddenly speeded up so much that it was obvious that everyone else believed in this sultan business.

Throughout the journey the princess, as a member of the palace of a neighboring country, talked about the difficulties they had had with this country until now. At one point she said something that really astounded Yağmur:

"My Sultan, whenever we made an offer for agreement, the Rain Country Administration always refused."

"What country did you say?"

"Rain Country! Why? Did I say something wrong?"

"No, please continue," he said but later on he would never remember what she had said, because he didn't listen to a word.

They arrived at the city close to sunset. Returning to their homes, people looked curiously at the palace coach and tried to understand who was in it. Some said:

"Ah! Isn't this the neighboring country's princess, Stranger Sultan?"

But none of them recognized Yağmur. When they came to the front of the palace, things suddenly reversed. From the moment Yağmur stepped out of the carriage, all the employees working in the service of the palace greeted him with looks of amazement and bowed heads:

"Welcome my Sultan!"

When he went towards the entrance door, he saw workers who were trying to remove the writing and who did not notice him. He quickly went to their sides and appearing as serious as he could, he said:

"Immediately stop removing that writing. When I come I want to see it polished."

Two of the workers fell off the ladder and the rest said:

"At your command, our Sultan."

Yağmur said, "Take me to the large hall immediately," to a soldier waiting at attention a little further on. Passing through a zigzagging corridor where everyone who saw him was plastered to the wall with respect, they arrived at the great hall. The guard at the door was about to inform those inside the hall, but he froze with the sign, "Don't speak." Yağmur slowly opened the door and, without attracting any attention, he stood behind the soldiers waiting at the threshold of the door. There was a commander in front of the soldiers giving an explanation to Sir Ego:

"Sir, as you ordered, we brought the caravan of food to the city yesterday. There are twenty-one men, six women (four of which are young), seventy-two camels and a lot of food, sir. What do you command we do with them?"

"I guess you haven't yet heard our saying, 'What comes with lust, goes with lust.' In this case, all the things you listed are your booty. Only those two old women won't be of any good to you. Put them among the slaves here."

"Do you have any other commands, sir?"

"Tell Commander Anger to send a couple of his soldiers to get those slaves," Sir Ego said. Turning towards the slaves, he stated:

"Because of you we still have not been able to remove the entrance writing. And wherever you found him, you helped this old man. Look, you made him miserable, too."

After Yağmur bent down among the soldiers and curiously looked at the slaves, he began to walk towards Sir Ego saying "*Ya Bismallah!*"

## Either Victory or Death

There was not a single sound. Everyone was watching the Sultan with eyes wide-open. Yağmur did the best thing he could have done: without saying a word, he sat down on his throne, the symbol of power. Also, thus, he was able to easily see who would obey him and who would rebel against him.

The situation was much better than he thought it would be. While all the palace officials—Sir Conscience and Servant to begin with—came before him and pledged their obedience, Sir Ego remained the last. Even though it was obvious that he didn't want to, he came forward and greeted the Sultan. Yağmur was still not talking; if he had, he would not be this effective. His sitting silently on the throne put fear in hearts and everyone waited curiously for his first words. Actually, because he was aware of this, he didn't want to say anything wrong and spoil this atmosphere.

When everyone took their place and, sitting motionless, focused their eyes on him, he understood that he needed to speak. But, of course, being a sultan was not something he did on a daily basis. Or he did it, but wasn't aware of it. His first words were as follows:

"From this moment on there is martial law in Rain Country. Until things return to normal, no one including Grand Vizier Ego has the authority to make decisions or give commands. All decisions and commands must carry my seal. Sir Conscience, I am appointing you as supervisor to Sir Ego during this period. Sir Intelligence, you are not going to work with anyone but me. As for you, Commander Lust! You are no different from Sir Ego. Know that from this moment on if not only you, but any of your soldiers take a step without my orders, I will exile you and your whole army to the 'Desert of Fasting.' Meanwhile, immediately remove from here those alcohol and gambling tables."

The Sultan continued:

"Tell me, Sir Ego, how long ago was I thrown into prison?"

"Approximately fifteen years ago, my Sultan."

"Can you dare such a thing again?"

"In truth, this is up to you, my Sultan."

Yağmur paused a minute when he heard this answer. He chose to think a little rather than getting angry. He said to himself:

"Approximately fifteen years. This is just about the time when my grandfather died. Of course, at the same time it is when the days of my youth began and I left aside everything including my Prayers and began living heedlessly.

So that's what he means by 'This is up to you." It would be wrong for me to become angry."

"Sir Conscience! Why don't I see any mosques in our city?"

"Forgive me, Sultan, but the mosque your deceased grandfather made was razed by the Grand Vizier years ago. We were not able to stop him, sir."

"Was it about fifteen years ago?"

"Yes, sir."

"Meanwhile, I am making Servant my 'Assistant Administrator'" Yağmur said, but no one seemed to understand. He immediately corrected himself:

"I mean I am making him my 'Special Advisor." Of course, if he will accept."

"Of course, my Sultan, it is an honor for me."

"Then your first job is to inspect Sir Ego's room. I will be very happy if you take his office keys and several soldiers with you and make an inspection. Also, please take the keys to the desk drawers. You will need them."

Sir Ego was astounded. After extending the keys, with a very red face, to Servant, he was just leaving the hall, but Yağmur did not ignore his first rebellion. Saying "Permission to leave was not given, Sir Ego," he felt he was speaking their language.

"I would also like to learn the name of the employee you spoke with this morning."

"Master Spirit, it was just an ordinary worker."

"I asked his name, Sir Ego."

"Umm... Waswas (Evil Suggestor), my Sultan."

Yağmur immediately called out to two soldiers there:

"Hurry and catch the evil insinuator named Waswas and throw him into prison. I'll deal with him later. As for you, Sir Ego! My first punishment for you is to build a large mosque just next to the palace. You will work together with the laborers. In addition, I want to see you in the front line at every ritual Prayer."

"I'll begin tomorrow morning, sir."

"No, Sir Ego! You will begin immediately. I am warning you openly: if you act according to your own pleasure and not in the way I command, I will exile you to the Desert of Fasting where bread and water are a mirage. Then I will cut off your friendship with your two valuable men, Sleep and Comfort. If this is not enough, I will relieve you of your position as Grand Vizier and make you a toilet cleaner. I swear by God I will do all of this!"

The oath the Sultan swore at the end of his words came down like a sledgehammer on Sir Ego's head. It was very important in regard to expressing the seriousness of the situation. The Sultan would not break an oath that he had made in front of this many people! As soon as Sir Ego and his natural inspector, Sir Conscience, left to work, Servant entered hastily.

"The news is not good, my Sultan," he said.

"What's happening, Servant? I've never seen you this upset."

"I found the letters Azazel sent Sir Ego. Putting aside the previous ones, today's letter requires that we take urgent precaution. See for yourself," Servant said.

The letter he extended to the Sultan read as follows:

"From Azazel, the rebel cursed by God, an apprehension to my valuable friend and future vizier, Sir Ego,

I don't have the patience to wait for the writing on the entrance to the palace to be removed. I am known for my hastiness. For this reason, I am preparing my armies. We will set out with the second rising of the sun. We are going to make an invasion unlike any that has ever been seen before.

As for your role in this great attack: You will not inform the palace administration about this in any way and you will not oppose my army. It will be good for both of us if this is an easy victory. Take good care of my throne and just keep it empty for two more days.

May God's wrath and damnation be upon you!

Commander-in-Chief of the Armies of Evil, Azazel"

Yağmur had not been sitting on the throne for even a half an hour when he had begun to be confronted with the greatest difficulties a sultan could have.

"Since he said the second rising of the sun, that means we have two nights left. How can an army be prepared in this short a time?"

"My first recommendation is to leave the Army of Lust out of this war. They can quickly fall into the traps of Azazel's army. Together with this, if we can release Commander Anger's hatred against Azazel and his army, it will be very helpful to us in this war."

"How can we do that?"

"The thing that angers Commander Anger the most is playing with his pride. If we say that Azazel considers him to be a commander who doesn't understand anything about war, is worth nothing, and is a coward and that if Azazel wins this war, he will treat him like a slave who cleans his boots, it will suffice to put Commander Anger into action."

"Very smart! How do you know these things?"

Answering, "My Sultan, this is not the first time I am acting as an 'Assistant Administrator,'" Servant chuckled in regard to this expression.

"What else can we do?"

"Of course, there is your most effective vizier, Sir Intelligence. If you can manage him correctly, he will be very helpful to you throughout the whole war. But I have to say that these will not be enough."

"I guess not. We saw before how dangerous Azazel and his army can be. Don't you have any other ideas?"

"Of course! I left the thing that will ease you most until the end. Do you remember that when we first met I mentioned a Combatants' Unit tied to the Warriors' Unit?"

"The ones who fight directly with the enemy?"

"Absolutely! With the a little help from the Combatants' Unit, our army will be ready."

"OK, but how are we going to ask for this help?"

"You have to inform all the people and speed-up the construction of the mosque."

If everyone knows how serious the situation is, what will happen to them if this war is lost, and what a hell Rain Country will become under Azazel's captivity, they will obey all your commands. Repentance and pleading to be made all together in the mosque that will be completed as soon as possible will be evaluated by the Holy Sphere and can allow a command to be given to the Combatants' Unit."

"Understood. In this case, you take care of the part related to the armies of Anger and Lust. I'll immediately speak to the people."

Saying, "You are truly a good sultan," Servant was happy with his whole being to give support to Yağmur.

The word "Sultan" must have called up an association for Yağmur because before leaving, he said laughingly to Servant, "You owe me an explanation about the empty prison."

Saying, "It will be my first job after the war," Servant took off his ring and extended it to Yağmur:

"If you accept it, I would like for this ring to be your seal," he said.

Yağmur's eyes filled with tears as he took the ring and looked at it.

There was a black stone in the middle of the ring and a word written around it: SERVANT. This ring was the sign of a more important position than the sultanate. It was more valuable than the throne he sat on, more meaningful than the life he lived and more amazing than all his dreams. With the ring on his finger, he was now officially a Servant.

# Preparations Begin

With one command, Yağmur wanted all the people to gather in front of the palace. The time being midnight was very appropriate in regard to expressing the importance of what he was going to say. While people slowly began to gather, he had an opportunity to think well about what he was going to say. After all, this was going to be his first address to the people as a sultan. When news came that everyone was ready and he took his place on the balcony facing the broad palace courtyard, the drone of the crowd suddenly ceased. Now the sultan was going to speak.

When he said, "My dear people. With the exception of palace officials, I don't believe that any of you have seen me before. I am aware that I have neglected you too much until now and I am very sorry for this. However, my reason for gathering you together here at this time of night is not just to be with you, but to warn you of a rapidly approaching danger," a droning noise rose from the crowd.

He continued:

"Approximately thirty-six hours later the greatest enemy that can appear in the history of mankind and his huge army will attack our country. It is such an army that it has devastated almost every country it has entered and, like a swarm of grasshoppers, it did not leave until it had dried up all the resources of the land. Leaving only blood, tears and smoke behind, this vile army's next target is us." The droning was replaced by screams.

"Now I want you to listen to me very carefully. I have just been reunited with you. I have no intention of leaving without feeling your love in my heart, giving attention to your problems, easing your pain or wiping away the tears from your eyes. In this case, today this is an opportunity not for disaster, but for our becoming one collective body. If you do what I say, I swear to God that we will bury that vile enemy in the 'Valley of Faith.'"

When the crowd heard this, it was as if they were grabbing on with their lives to a rope extended to them just as they were about to drown, and they shouted all together:

"Command, our Sultan! Command, our Sultan! We will do as you want."

Sultan Yağmur continued:

"Then the first thing to be done is to finish the construction of the mosque being built in the palace courtyard. Tomorrow night we will all gather together in this mosque and ask forgiveness for the sins we have committed so far. I am speaking openly: without God's help, we can do nothing before such an army whose swords are from fire, whose horses breathe smoke, and whose screams are an earthquake. If we do what we should, God will help us with soldiers from the Combatants' Unit."

The people felt a little relief. At that moment someone from the crowd called out to the Sultan:

"Our Sultan, if you see fit, we would also like to support you with our army."

The person all eyes were turned upon was Stranger Sultan. She continued:

"Your neighbor, my father, "Honorable Friend," will be happy to help you in this struggle."

Yağmur courteously accepted this thoughtful offer:

"We would be happy to accept the help of Honorable Friend. You can set out immediately with ten armed cavalrymen to accompany you. The faster your army comes, the better it will be. We don't have much time to determine our tactics."

Meanwhile, the crowd was a little more relieved by the assistance to come and they voiced their gladness:

"Long live our Sultan! Long live our Sultan!"

When Yağmur said, "Let's go, distinguished people of Rain Country! Let's get started immediately," everyone began to run.

Despite the darkness of the night and all their weariness, these people with hopeful hearts carried rocks, brought sand and transported water. With the participation of the Sultan among them, the scene was complete. It was as if the first masjid was being built in Medina.

With the first morning rays of light, Servant came close to Yağmur. It was so obvious that he was bothered by something, but didn't want to make the Sultan sad by telling him that Yağmur, unable to endure the situation, asked:

"I hope everything is OK. I am not very accustomed to seeing you apprehensive."

"We have a serious problem, Yağmur."

"Please tell me! What is it?"

"We cannot fight Azazel and his army with the swords we have. When I came to rescue you from Azazel, you saw that I killed one of the devils there, didn't you?"

"Yes, you had a deep blue sword in your hand."

"That sword was made from a very special metal. It is able to endure the heat of the fluid that flows in the veins of the devils that are created from fire. Of course, it is not possible for us to find it here. However, at least we can increase the durability of our swords by coating them with a kind of ice."

"But how? I have no knowledge about this at all."

"You don't need to understand. Do you remember what I said while we were coming here? Viziers rule countries; they are ruled by sultans. Think about this a little, if you like." Servant picked up the rock he had put on the ground and left.

Yağmur remained frozen among the thousands of people who were coming and going like an ant colony. Was he going to think about coating the swords with ice or about governing the viziers? Or was he going to leave the task of thinking to the viziers? Well, wasn't it Sir Intelligence's job to think? He immediately began to look excitedly for Sir Intelligence. Of course, Servant was watching him from the corner of his eye and laughingly saying, "This child truly resembles his grandfather."

Yağmur began to speak as soon as he found Sir Intelligence:

Sir Intelligence! I want our existing swords to be plated with ice. It should be as cold as possible. Do you have any ideas?"

"Let me think about it; I'll find a way, my Sultan."

"Don't take too long, because you know we don't have much time."

Saying "Immediately, sir," Sir Intelligence began to run towards the palace. Yağmur was going to see the ironsmiths to see what stage the swords they were making were in when he saw that Sir Ego had entered the palace alone. It was obvious that he was not going to correct his bad temperament. He followed him to the prison underneath the palace. He had just ordered the soldier on duty to release Waswas when Yağmur shouted to the soldier as loud as he could:

"Wait a minute, soldier! Stop fooling with that door and immediately arrest Sir Ego."

The soldier did what he was commanded and seized the Grand Vizier by his arms.

"What were you going to do after freeing Waswas, Sir Ego? Were you going to send him to Azazel? Were you going to inform him of our preparations? Obviously, you did not believe the oaths I made yesterday. Do you think I will not ban you to the Fasting Desert? Then there is just one way for you to believe me."

When Yağmur said, "Soldier, bring Sir Ego here," the Grand Vizier finally understood that the sultan was not the old sultan. But this had to be a lesson he wouldn't forget.

Calling Sir Conscience as soon as he went outside, Yağmur gave him a directive:

"Sir Conscience, quickly leave Sir Ego in the middle of the Fasting Desert and bring his horse back."

"At your command, sir."

Yağmur had calculated that by acting like this he would encourage Sir Ego to gather himself together and, at the same time, he wouldn't have to supervise him throughout the war.

Just as it was getting dark, suddenly clouds of dust covered the horizon. While everyone dropped what they were doing and thought about how they could be saved from a sudden attack, Yağmur shouted in a tone of surrender to faith:

"Don't worry! Everyone should continue his work."

The extent of the approaching cloud of dust gave an approximate idea of the power of the approaching army. Saying, "This must be the army of Honorable Friend," he was very relieved when he saw someone in the small scouting party whose clothing indicated he was a sultan. The woman beside him must be Stranger Sultan. Yağmur immediately proceeded towards the city entrance gate to personally meet these helpful neighbors.

Then he accompanied them to the palace with their servants so they could rest. At that time Sir Intelligence was coming out of the palace.

He said:

"I have found it. I have found it, sir." The guests became very curious.

Sir Intelligence said:

"Sir, I would be very happy if you would come to the laboratory." They all followed him inside.

As soon as Sir Intelligence poured a blue fluid giving off steam onto a piece of iron, it became ice with crackling sounds coming from the iron. While Sir Intelligence was trying to let go of the iron that had stuck to his hand due to his excitement, Yağmur briefly explained the situation to Honorable Friend. The amazed looks of the guests were still on the frozen iron in Sir Intelligence's hand. After that they went to their rooms to rest.

As Yağmur was about to go outside from the labyrinth-like corridors that he had learned in a short time, the sound he heard made him freeze in his tracks. He had longed to hear this voice so much:

"*Allahu Akbar, Allahu Akbar...*" This sound was worth all this trouble. He excitedly flew outside. Someone had stood on the wall of the mosque under construction, which had only risen to the height of a person, and brought to an end fifteen years of yearning and fifteen years of heedlessness. It was as if he was rending the bosom of darkness with the dagger of "*Allahu Akbar, Allahu Akbar...*"

Yağmur would never forget this Evening Prayer in which he led thousands of worshipers. Wasn't everything for this? What was the meaning of all that had happened if not to stand in His presence and say, *Iyyaka na'budu wa iyyaka nastain* (You alone do We worship, and from You alone do we seek help). It was as if everything ended at that moment. At the moment when every individual in Rain Country expressed his servanthood, it was as if it was the end of everything because the purpose was this. Or just the opposite, it was the moment that everything was beginning. It was beginning with an enemy they had made because they expressed their servanthood to God.

Just like Adam, just like Able, just like Abraham and his family. Because they said, "I serve only You and ask for help only from You," tomorrow morning they would confront the most evil, most merciless, most vile and most powerful enemy. But God, whom they had just bowed down to on the Prayer mat, had made a promise:

"Use your voice to move them internally as much as you have the power to; become partners to their goods and children; make promises to them... But what can a devil promise but deceit? I have some true servants; you have no dominion over them. Their Lord suffices them as advocate before your deceits against them."

In that Evening Prayer, Yağmur relived all the things that had occurred throughout his journey that had begun with Servant. The enemy was the same enemy, but this time it was not Abraham, Hagar or Ishmael before the enemy, but Yağmur. And, of course, the never changing and always existent advocate God, may He be honored and glorified. Now who would fear the vile Azazel and his army?

After the Evening Prayer, all preparations were made. With the repentance and prayers made after the Night Prayer, everyone began to wait for the morning.

# When Is God's Help?

After acting as sultan and imam for forty-eight hours, it was time for Yağmur to become commander. With the Morning Prayer they performed, he was at the front of the army headed towards the Valley of Faith. The information they got from Waswas, whom they held captive, showed that Azazel and his army would come from this direction. Occasionally looking behind him, Yağmur wanted to be sure that everything was alright. Another matter that was keeping his mind busy was when the Combatant soldiers would arrive.

Riding a white horse, Servant was just next to Yağmur. On his other side was the sultan of the neighboring country, Honorable Friend. Behind him Sir Intelligence, Sir Conscience, Commander Anger and the other palace officials took their places. Commander Anger's soldiers comprised the right flank of the army, and Honorable Friend's soldiers the left flank. The position of the middle division, thought to be the main force, was still vacant. Yağmur acted like this to show his faith in God's help and his surrender to it. Only Servant and Sir Conscience were not uneasy with this situation. They fully believed that God would be their "advocate" in this struggle.

When with the first rays of the sun Yağmur looked at the Valley of Faith, he saw an army that was unaware of what kind of power would confront them, but who would never turn their backs to that force. Seeing that waiting silently created tension for the soldiers, Yağmur spoke to them with the hope of relieving them a little:

"My soldiers! Today two armies will face each other in this field. One of these will fight for honor, freedom, faith and victory; the other will fight for darkness, pride, damnation and defeat. Even this sun you see rose to watch the struggle between faith and unbelief. Even if it saw many battles and many epics before under the names of Nimrud and Abraham, peace be upon him, the Pharaoh and Moses, peace be upon him, the Quraysh and Muhammad, peace and blessings be upon him, and even if it knew many heroes like Hamza, Khalid, Ali, Umar, Salahaddin and Fatih, it came today to see a new epic and to know new heroes. I swear to you that when evening comes, this sun will not leave the Valley of Faith with its head down! It will not set before it has seen the epic it awaits and before it has met the heroes who will write this epic!"

The whole army was incited. The Valley of Faith was resounding with the cries of "*Allahu Akbar*!" when they saw that a darkness more like smoke than a cloud of dust was approaching towards them full speed. Together with Commander Anger and Honorable Friend immediately moving to take their places at the head of their armies, the command to pour the special liquid prepared by Sir Intelligence was heard. While all the soldiers looked with amazement as their swords were all suddenly coated with ice, Yağmur approached Servant:

"When do think help will come?" he asked.

Servant replied with a verse from the Quran:

"*Ala, inna nasrallahi qarib*!" (For certain God's help is near!).

Yağmur was so relieved with this answer that he began to ride his horse at a gallop with no hesitation. Not understanding what suddenly happened, the soldiers, seeing their commander riding towards the enemy alone, spurred their horses immediately and followed him shouting *takbir*.[6]

This sudden movement enabled the enemy to understand a reality they were not expecting: before them there was not a country waiting to surrender, but an army determined to chase them to Hell. Calculating that he would be sitting on the throne at most a half an hour later, Azazel didn't know what to do when he was confronted by an army pointing their swords at him and galloping forward fearlessly. They almost didn't bring their swords so they wouldn't have to carry the weight, but now invading this country without swinging their swords was just a fantasy. The only thing they had been able to do was to pull out their swords when they came face-to-face with the fearless warriors.

---

[6] Saying *Allahu Akbar* (God is the Greatest).

The first hot contact with the enemy took place at the tip of the icy swords. While Yağmur tried to reach Azazel whom he had met before by eliminating all the devils in front of him, Servant tried to protect him without ever leaving his side. He was the first to taste the unbearable pain of the swords of fire. When he saw four devils swooping down on Yağmur at the same time in order to eliminate him, he immediately threw himself in front of Yağmur. While struggling with two of them, he was only able to act as a shield against the other two.

The absence of the middle forces began to create a big problem. Commander Anger and Honorable Friend were trying with all their might to press the enemy in their own flanks, but having found an easy way to escape, the enemy slowly slid towards the middle... where there were no forces. When Yağmur remained with just a group of warriors comprised of his close aids, he was forced to ask Honorable Friend who was trying to make himself heard:

"Honorable Yağmur! Where is the help?"

He was asking this question no one knew the answer to because he had begun to lose his men three-five at a time. Just at that moment a cloud of dust coming swiftly towards the city gave hope to everyone.

Saying, "Help is on the way! Hang on, my warriors; help is coming," Yağmur was trying to protect wounded Servant more than reach Azazel. The good side of the situation was that the coming help had begun to put a smile on everyone's face.

On the one hand, Sir Conscience was trying to cover Yağmur's back and, on the other hand, he was trying to see out of the corner of his eye who this approaching help was. He was the first to frown. Because the approaching division was Sir Ego, Commander Lust and his army. If he didn't know Sir Ego so well, he could have thought he was coming to help. But he knew there was no probability of this. The only thing he could do was to warn everyone at the same time:

"The enemy is coming from behind... the enemy is coming from behind."

Those who could look in spite of the swords of fire were totally smashed by what they saw. Yes, as if Azazel and his huge army were not enough, now they had to fight with their own army as well.

They had been betrayed in the full meaning of the word. They were caught between two fires. Even Yağmur's strength had begun to be sapped. The mid-ranks had not been left empty for them. It was one thing to face an enemy many times more powerful than themselves, to attack them single-handedly, and to fight with several devils at the same time. But when he saw the Grand Vizier with a sword in his hand coming to kill him, his hands fell to his side. Seeing him like this, Servant whispered to him in a weak voice as if he were teaching his dear student one last thing:

"This door's entrance is from within. Don't you dare allow them in this door!"

Although Yağmur did not understand at that moment, he remembered the first time he saw those words. It was written underneath some other writing on the entrance door to the palace.

They were such words that many Yağmurs had been lost for its sake until now. They were such words that the reign of innumerable oppressors had been destroyed. They were such words that those who spoke them became the Companions of the blessed Prophet:

"*La ilaha illallah. Muhammadu'r-Rasulullah*!"

These blessed words that Yağmur shouted at the top of his voice began to be repeated by the whole army as if it were a command. So much so that all the devils seemed to be looking for a place to escape from these words. It was as if time had stopped, space had evaporated and life had come to an end in the Valley of Faith which was echoing with these words... until everything came to life again with the sound of "*Allahu Akbar*! *Allahu Akbar*!"

The face of the person who was calling *takbir* in front of the army approaching with illumination that would overpower the darkness brought by Azazel and his army was familiar to Yağmur. The one commanding this army of angels was none other than Azazel's undefeated rival, Abraham. Having dragged his one and only student after him all the way here, Servant responded to Abraham at this awaited moment saying "*La ilaha illallahu wallahuakbar*!" (There is no deity but God, and He is the Greatest). Having convinced this many people who trusted him to confront the enemy with God's promise of help, Yağmur expressed his gratitude with these words of completion: "*Allahu Akbar wa lillahil hamd!*" (God is the Greatest, and all praise be for God).

While Abraham and his army cut down the enemy army with the swords of light in their hands, Yağmur and his army took the opportunity to repel the traitors attacking them from the rear, and they took Sir Ego and Commander Lust as captives.

When they turned around, nothing remained but thousands of dead devils and a few who were still in the process of dying. There was no trace of either Abraham or Azazel. While the whole army was calling *takbir* in joy, Yağmur was looking at the horizon with eyes still filled with curiosity and he was trying to understand what had happened.

## What Actually Happened?

The army returning with victory was joyously met by all the people in the city. While everyone was returning to his home in peace after a weariness that had continued constantly for two days, Sultan Yağmur, for whom resting was just a dream, was thinking about things to be done. In particular, Sir Ego was at the top of the list of things on his mind. For the first time in days he was able to remain alone in the grand hall with Servant, and now everything needed to be brought out in the open.

Yağmur began the talk:

"What do you say to beginning with the things that happened in the Cave of Heedlessness?"

When Servant remained suddenly confronted with such a question, he found it more appropriate to explain what happened from the beginning:

"I believe that you, too, understood these things to a certain extent. You were the sultan of this country from the start. The first phase of the Power Vacuum Period I mentioned to you was the first four months you spent in your mother's womb. Grand Vizier Sir Ego, your first cell that began to form the moment you were conceived in your mother's womb, and then the others were the citizens of this country. During these four months until you were sent to this country as Master Spirit, each cell recognized Sir Ego and obeyed him. As a sultan, you only needed to govern Sir Ego. Sir Conscience was appointed to help you with this task. It was his job to always speak the truth with the inspiration he received from the angels. Years later another assistant, Sir Intelligence came. You were approximately twelve years-old then. It was his duty to show you which of the things Sir Ego wanted to implement in the country were right and which were wrong. In order to meet the needs of the people and to protect them from danger, Commanders Lust and Anger, together with their armies, would help you."

"Everything seems to be OK until here," Yağmur added. But Servant did not agree:

"Not really. Sir Ego began a number of tasks according to his own wishes. Just as he did not hesitate to use his position just for the things he wanted, he also began to get upset from time to time with some of your commands. For example, you wanted him to perform Prayers, but he hated it. You wanted him to fast, but hunger and thirst spoiled his pleasure. You prohibited one of his greatest entertainments, gambling, and his joy of living was extinguished. Saying 'fornication is forbidden,' you hindered his desire for closeness with the opposite sex. You said, 'Lying, talking behind someone's back, gossiping and cursing are forbidden!' and he didn't have anything left to say. You said, 'There will be no envy, pride, wrath or oppression!' and you hit him in his most vital place. In other words, you tried to prohibit his desires and make into law things he didn't want, so the first thing he did regarding this was to incite Commanders Anger and Lust against you."

Servant continued explaining:

"Then one day, when Azazel's messenger Waswas came and began to bring a number of suggestions, he really went wild. Because Azazel was promising all his desires. Of course, with one condition: 'Get rid of Master Spirit, put me on the throne and see how you will get the life you want!' He learned from Azazel how to handle Sir Conscience, how to make Sir Intelligence work for his own account and, worst of all, how to put you on the road to prison without your being aware of it. And you were taken in by this game. In particular, your bad friendship with Sleep and Comfort put you on the road to prison in the Cave of Heedlessness. It was the same scenario for Azazel, but for you it was very different. Many sultans were pulled into the same game by their grand viziers. Some were lost in the Cave of Heedlessness like you, some were exiled to the Gambling Mountain and some disappeared while chained in the Swamp of Fornication. It only remained to Azazel to mount the empty thrones."

"You're so right. While passing through the swamps and mountains you mentioned, I left many of my friends there. They got stuck and remained there. Thanks to God, you saved me from the Cave of Heedlessness. But now I remember that when I asked whether or not Sir Ego would have the courage to do this again, you said, 'It's up to you!' In other words, there will always be this risk." With the idea of executing Sir Ego still in his mind, Yağmur asked, "How can I be saved from him?"

Servant answered as if he had understood Yağmur's thoughts:

"I told you this before, Yağmur; you will not get anyplace by killing Sir Ego. In addition, this is contrary to the rules of the game. Why should he be killed? To load all your work on his back? Actually that Grand Vizier of yours has much better merits than you think."

This time Yağmur was really surprised:

Saying, "Of course not. Uhh... Forgive me! What I wanted to say is that it never occurred to me that he had any virtues," Yağmur's astonishment was very obvious.

"Of course, it is normal for you to be this much surprised, for you haven't yet seen his good side. But this has a little bit to do with your perspective. Think of it this way: If Sir Ego has set his mind on something, he will do it. You will not be able to see a more stubborn, persistent and desirous creature than him in your life. The only problem is his wanting things that will make him regretful in the end. He resembles a child in this respect. Children also want things that can harm them, but no parent has killed their child for this. In that case, the thing you need to do is not to execute Sir Ego, but to train him."

"But you know how I exiled him to the Desert of Fasting and how he escaped from there. What else can I do?"

"If you suddenly cut off all the comfort and bounteousness he has grown accustomed to over the years, of course, you will make him rebel. However, in times like this it is necessary to take action gradually, step by step. Instead of sending him to the Desert of Fasting at first, you could have begun by making a change in his daily banquet table. If he is coming and going to tables full of many different foods six times a day, the first thing to do is to decrease the variety of the food. If you do it like this, you will put him in a certain discipline without making him rebel. The same thing is true for sleep. Accustomed for years to ten hours of pleasure on feather beds, Sir Ego can be disciplined by slowly decreasing his hours of sleep. Growing accustomed in time to the program you have made for him, Sir Ego will get used to living with your rules after some time. Later on I am going to explain in detail the matters of eating and sleeping. Now we have to take care of pressing matters and go."

"What kind of things are you talking about?"

"There is a very important reason for Sir Ego's rebelling against you: the source he is nurtured from. When we first came to the city together, you must have seen five large rivers emptying into the lake just behind the palace. All the people of the city, including Sir Ego, are nourished from the water of the lake and from animals and plants benefitting from that water. These rivers are the Eye River,

Tongue River, Ear River, Stomach River and Hand-Foot River."

Servant continued:

"With the poison he poured into these rivers for years, Azazel succeeded in gradually making all the people sick. None of them can think straight, make correct decisions or choose between what is good or bad for themselves. How do you think they were entering that city of alcohol that they called Fountain?"

He added:

"The first thing we need to do is to set up a purification plant. We will not use anything coming from outside without it being purified in this facility which we will call the 'Repentance Purification Plant.' At a later step we will place soldiers specially trained by Sir Ego every ten meters up to the sources of these five rivers. They will not allow any barrel labeled 'Sin, inc.' to be thrown into these rivers. Of course, together with all these, you are a Servant. There are things you have to do in the outside world and you should not neglect them. At any rate, that was the reason why I said we have to go immediately."

When Servant said this, Yağmur began to feel a little uncomfortable and said:

"OK, but can't I first finish my work as sultan in my inner world and then set out to the outer world?"

"No, that's not possible. Many others think like you, but this is another kind of Azazel's trickery. Think about it. What would have happened if the sultan of the neighboring country, Honorable Friend, had said, 'I haven't finished my inner work yet! I'll take care of it later!' instead of coming to help us and had left us alone in our struggle with Azazel?"

Saying, "A Servant will strive both to put his own inner issues in order and to find people who will "serve" his external world, help him in his struggle with Azazel, and support him against Sir Ego's treachery," he continued with his explanation:

"This order you saw in your inner world is the same internally for everyone. They also each have a Sir Ego, Sir Conscience, Sir Intelligence, and Commanders Lust and Anger. Only their sultans and the places of the prisons where they are held captive are different. Just as I helped you today to escape from your imprisonment and take your place on the throne, you should help people in the same way to sit on their thrones in their inner worlds."

Then he made an important reminder:

"Before going, there is one more thing: You should never leave this throne during the day. If you turn to your inner world and see that you have strayed from your throne, immediately sit there and look at what is happening in the country. Especially, don't ever take your eyes off Sir Ego. For he will take every opportunity in your absence to rule the country according to his own pleasure. He will make contact somehow with Azazel and they will plan a way to send you to prison. Whenever you feel that you have strayed from the throne, immediately say, '*La ilaha illa'llah, Muhammadu'r-Rasulullah!*' and close your eyes. In this way your entrance will be from within just as was written on the door. At that moment you will see what is going on in the palace and as long as you look at life from this throne, you will be aware of what you are living every moment and you will take precautions accordingly. Actually what everyone now calls "being present" is this. Shah an-Naqshband called this state *Khush dar dam* (self-breathing, awareness of Divine presence). At any rate, as I said before, we'll get into detailed matters regarding your inner world later on. In addition, you can enter other palaces where the writing has not yet been removed from the entrance door. Now there are people who are waiting for help and you need to learn which qualities you need to possess in order to help them. You don't need to come to your grave to do this! I will be with you on this path which is new to you in every journey you will make during the day to your own palace or to someone else's palace. I entrust you to God and do not leave the throne vacant."

When Yağmur recited the chapter An-Nas and opened his eyes, it was still light out. Suddenly his mental concept of time was turned upside-down. Saying, "What day is today? What time...Oh, I don't have a watch! Wait a minute... I'll understand in a minute," he began to walk. When he arrived at the cemetery gate and saw that it was locked, he thought that it must still be Sunday morning...

## Come and Meet Dasim!

It was approaching 9:00 a.m. when he arrived home. It was early to wake someone up on Sunday morning, but the promise he had made to his mother two weeks ago changed everything. He liked to call this Ottoman lady, who was even more authoritarian than his father, "Valide Sultan" (Mother Sultan). The biggest problem right now was that he hadn't informed his wife of this promise. In this fast tempo he had even forgotten himself. The best way would be to wake up Rehnüma with some other excuse and mention the breakfast issue later.

Yağmur was very surprised when he realized that he had consulted with his viziers on even such a simple matter as this. The inner voices were so familiar that who said what was immediately recognizable:

Sir Ego: "In my opinion the best thing to do is to immediately go to bed and sleep. We'll tell Valide Sultan that we weren't able to wake up."

Sir Conscience: "What do you mean? This would clearly be a lie. Plus there is a given promise."

Sir Intelligence: "I think that Sir Conscience is right. In addition, if we don't go, Valide Sultan will make us pay for it."

Sir Ego: "But won't Rehnüma get upset? Let's say we wake her up now and say, 'Come on, we're going to my mother's!' She will have a frown on her face until evening. The best thing to do is to curl up beside her and go to sleep. You're very tired anyway. Come on, let's not lose time. The bed is waiting for us."

Sir Conscience: "I also know that Rehnüma is going to get angry in this situation. However, Sir Intelligence will find a solution. In the end, the important thing is to keep our word without making anyone angry."

Sir Intelligence: "What's easier than this? We'll wake her up for another reason and then mention the promise we made two weeks ago. Without giving her a chance to get mad, if we offer to stop at the market on the way home and pick up what's needed, then everything will be fine.

Honorable Yağmur: "How clever. This is the best idea!"

Sir Intelligence: "It was nothing, my Sultan. That's my job..."

Yağmur set to work.

"Rehnüma! Where's the tea? I can't find it."

"Why do you ask? You usually don't make tea."

"My dear, you have been making breakfast for years. Why don't I make it for once?"

"I hope everything is OK. The tea is in the cupboard above the stove. Be careful not to spill it on the floor'"

"I can't guarantee it. You know I'm not very skillful in the kitchen."

"It's obvious you're not going to let me sleep. Hold on a minute and I'll prepare breakfast."

"Speaking of breakfast, I just remembered! How could I forget it? About two weeks ago while I was talking with Valide Sultan on the phone..."

...

They had set out on the road, but Rehnüma was still downcast. Yağmur, on the other hand, was dignified and calm as if he were sitting on the palace throne rather than a car seat. He no longer got mad about the things that used to anger him. He knew very well what kind of trouble people had with their egos. Knowing the trip that passed silently to be booty, he began to think:

"Actually we expect a lot from people. All these expectations are due to our assuming that they are as a sultan sitting on his throne and ruling the physical country. But actually we are only conversing with the grand vizier of a country in which who knows what prison the sultan is held. We get very upset when we see unexpected things from him. For example, if I had not prevented Sir Ego from harming Stranger Sultan, who would her father Honorable Friend have held accountable? Me, of course. Then instead of helping against the enemy, he would have opposed me with all his power. In other words, we would all be sentenced for a crime Sir Ego committed."

"Actually we always act like this. A person in front of us has fully lost control to Sir Ego, his hands are tied, and he wants help from us. But instead of helping him, we declare war on the whole country due to Sir Ego's mistake. Actually, we show enmity not to the evil in people's inner worlds, but to the poor ones who are the victims of that evil. We oppress the poor victims."

"As far as I can remember, it was in the Battle of Uhud... Our Prophet didn't even get angry with the polytheists of the Quraysh who threatened his life, broke his tooth and injured his face; he didn't curse them. To the contrary, on the one hand, he wiped the blood off his face and, on the other hand, he made this prayer: *Allahummaghfirli qawmi fa innahum la ya'lamun* (My God, spare my tribe! Because they do not know)."

"They were not aware of the torture that Azazel and their egos were taking them to as slaves. They did not know that the ego they served was only a vizier, that Satan who they thought was their friend was actually their enemy, and that they, themselves, were the sultan who could intervene and change everything. They did not know that by hanging on their palace door those blessed words, *La ilaha illallah. Muhammadu'r-Rasulullah*, and sitting on their own throne, they could be saved from all this slavery, vileness, corruption and treachery. Spare them, my Lord!"

Yağmur came to himself when Rehnüma said:

"Where are you going? You passed the street."

As if nothing had happened, he turned onto the next street, passed through a side street and stopped in front of the house. Even though he wasn't aware of how big a danger he had avoided by turning on that street instead of the previous one, he looked at his wife and said:

"There's a good side to everything."

The marvelous aroma beginning in front of the door was sufficient to understand how much trouble Valide Sultan had gone to. After kissing the hands of his mother and father, and being greeted as always by "you good-for-nothings," they all sat down at the table. Everything was going very well until that moment came that Yağmur had reluctantly expected. The first round of the Valide Sultan vs. Rehnüma match:

"You are still young and ignorant; you can't know. Wait until you are my age, then I'll see what you do!"

Rehnüma: ...

Yağmur became aware of the situation just in time. Before Rehnüma had said anything, he said, "If I hurry I can make it in time." Saying those blessed words, he closed his eyes.

According to what he saw, this definitely must be the palace in Rehnüma's heart. Many of the people in the grand hall were known to him at first glance. Yağmur thought for a moment about where he knew the people from. Oh yes! They were the actors in local television series. For example, this man in the black suit played in the "Dinner Table of the Wolves." Another one a little larger than him must be the adventurous young man in the "Hot Pepper" series. Those standing on the other side were all foreigners. There was an atmosphere as if they had come to an

Oscar Awards Ceremony. The problem was that Rehnüma Sultan, who was to present the awards, could not be seen. It was obvious why the throne was vacant. Who knows what "Black Box" the sultan of the country, Rehnüma, had been shut up in. Here the administration was in the hands of the grand vizier called Lady Ego. A messenger who came inside went and stood before the grand vizier. Just at that time, Yağmur heard Servant's voice:

"Do you recognize the messenger who came in?"

"Aaa...yes! Isn't that our Waswas?"

"That's right! He was sent by Dasim."

"Dasim? You never mentioned him before. Who is it?"

"The Army of Evil has its own kind of organization. At any rate, this army is as old as human history. In order to speed up his work, Azazel has distributed his duties to a certain extent. This is Dasim; the devils who incite members of the family, relatives and friends against one another are called Dasim. You will see the other groups later. Now let's see how Dasim does his job."

Then they listened to what Waswas had to say:

"Very esteemed Lady Ego! Since you made an alliance with the Yağmur Country years ago, the sultan of Valide Sultan Country, Valide Sultan, has constantly displayed a hostile attitude towards you. We have news of a new attack. Sir Dasim thinks that the best action to take is a sudden attack from the Tongue Road. Valide Sultan has accused you of ignorance. Sir Dasim wants you to finish the job here if necessary and to move with a strength that has not yet been seen. He wants you to know that the best card you have in your hand is the mistakes Valide Sultan made when she was young. May damnation be upon you lady!" Saying this Waswas left.

Yağmur had already begun his questions:

"My situation wasn't this bad. How can Waswas do his work so openly? He was much more cautious in my palace."

"Because you were a captive only in the Cave of Heedlessness. It could have been possible for you to escape from this heedlessness and awake from sleep at any moment. For this reason, they tried to do their work as secretly as possible without your knowing about it. But unfortunately the situation of your wife Rehnüma is much worse. It looks like they have put her in the Black Box. It is such a thing that not many people can escape safely. They live as if they have another life in the Black Box. Just as they don't feel they are captive, they forget their real life a little later. The only reality for them is the Black Box itself. This is one of Azazel's last traps. Ever since the Black Box appeared, his work has been lightened by half. So much so that it is sufficient to throw people in it. For they don't even have the intention of getting out."

Servant grew silent when one of the television stars in the hall began to speak. This impudent woman who was a speaker from one of the daily television programs for women seemed to be proving how successful she was at making agitation:

"Ma'am, ma'am! Don't you dare say you will take it humbly. If she says one thing to you, you say five to her. If she does one thing to you, you will make her regret it. Until today you have allowed yourself to be smashed; what good did it do? Are you more worthy now? From today on at least, you take the reins in your hand. No one has the right to oppress anyone else. That's it."

Then Lady Conscience took the floor:

"Look, Lady Ego, actually I think that Valide Sultan's words were misunderstood. I think what she wanted to say was: 'As your elder who has experienced some things you have not yet lived, I do not want you to make the same mistakes and be regretful like me when you are my age.' Consequently, just as there is no situation that requires an attack, thanks would even be appropriate." But Lady Ego did not agree at all. Lady Conscience was saying very nice and effective things, but a sultan who would listen to her was needed. Lady Ego immediately commanded Lady Intelligence:

"Lady Conscience, I want you to immediately set out with Commander Anger. You have to find whatever there is that we can use as trump cards. As soon as Commander Anger gets the necessary information, you should attack from the Tongue Road. Let me see your stuff; let's give this old woman a piece of her mind."

It happened just as she said. Rehnüma gave such an answer to Valide Sultan that everyone's mouth hung open, including her own:

"After all the silly things you did in your youth, I don't think you will live until I become your age! Today a feather bed, tomorrow a dirt bed..."

Everything was the same as always. When Valide Sultan got up from the table crying, everyone had played their role very well.

Now it was Yağmur's turn on the stage. Now it was his role to shout at Rehnüma and get revenge for his mother. However, after he saw what happened in the palace, he couldn't do this. He didn't want to be tricked by Dasim just like Lady Ego had been tricked. He immediately called out to Sir Intelligence from his throne:

"Sir Intelligence! What's the best thing to do now? I don't want anyone from my family to feel hurt or for that vile Dasim to be happy."

"Esteemed Sultan! First go to Valide Sultan who got up from the table and ease her heart. Tell her that Rehnüma truly acted ignorantly, that you are going to talk with her at home, that you apologize in her name, and that forgiving is the mature thing to do," said Sir Intelligence.

Lady Ego secretly put a piece of paper that she had just read into her pocket and then she interfered:

"Sir, in my opinion, what Sultan Rehnüma did was very shameful. It is your mother's right that you reprehend her here. You will make Valide Sultan very happy."

But Yağmur knew very well who he should really reprehend:

"Rather than Valide Sultan, might it not be the vile Dasim who will be happy here, Lady Ego? Either you burn that letter of insinuation in your pocket immediately or I will burn you."

As soon as he handled the internal matters as a sultan, Yağmur got up, comforted his mother's heart and had her sit at the table.

When they went home that evening, Yağmur looked for the right time to make a move. He knew very well that Lady Conscience had brought up the morning event again and again until evening. At every opportunity during the day he had monitored the palace in Rehnüma's heart and hadn't seen anyone to support this much complaining from Lady Conscience.

Yağmur remembered Azazel's letter that he had gotten a hold of previously. There Azazel had mentioned how important a force Sir Intelligence was and that he should never be brought together with Sir Conscience. In that case, what needed to be done was to convince Lady Intelligence. It was obvious that in this palace there was only one person who would pay attention to what Lady Ego said and that was Lady Intelligence! Yağmur found the chance to open this subject to his wife:

"Look, my dear Rehnüma! I am aware that you have been feeling sad all day because of the event that took place this morning. I am not going to question the right or wrong of what you did. But I know that you constantly are feeling regret. Believe me, apologizing to my mother will make you happy more than anyone else. Also, if you don't apologize, you will be bothered by it in both this world and the next. You know that Valide Sultan is close to seventy years-old. God forbid, that she passed away without your finding an opportunity to apologize. Due to the words you spoke this morning, you will feel pain as long as you live."

Then he added half-jokingly, "In my opinion, apologize; you'll see that you might get that overcoat you wanted on your birthday."

As if he was experimenting, Yağmur immediately went into Rehnüma's palace of the heart to see the effect of his words. The guard at the door of the grand hall called out inside:

"A messenger has come from our ally, Rain Country, lady!"

Saying, "Let him come and let's see what the mama's boy wants again," Lady Ego was unaware that he could hear these. The messenger turned directly to Lady Intelligence and began to read:

"Most esteemed Lady Intelligence, although you remained silent in regard to the events of this morning and their aftermath, I think that voicing your ideas would be beneficial for everyone. If you contemplate a little the complaints of Lady Conscience and explain them to Lady Ego, as your ally, I will be very happy.

Sultan of Rain Country, Honorable Yağmur."

Lady Intelligence listened one more time to what Lady Conscience said. Lady Conscience was saying the same things again and again:

"What else can I say besides what I said this morning. What we did was definitely wrong. Without listening to me, you attacked, so at least listen to me now. We need to apologize as soon as possible."

Hearing this, Lady Ego exploded:

"Enough of this! You have been saying the same things since morning. When I tell you to give a reason, you don't speak. Enough of this. Be quiet!"

Meanwhile, having the chance to think, Lady Intelligence immediately interrupted:

"Lady Ego, allow me to explain to you why we have to apologize. First of all, as long as we don't apologize, Lady Conscience will not be quiet, and I cannot endure her constant complaining. Secondly, we will have rejected the suggestion of our ally, Honorable Yağmur, and this can cause a problem for us in the future. He can reject our proposal in the future. But if we do what he wants, he will have to do the same for us. Thirdly, there is not much time left before the 'Birthday.' As you know, Valide Sultan sent congratulations with a very nice gift in the Birthday celebrations in the past. I don't think you would like to be deprived of this this year."

This was just the language Lady Ego understood. She immediately gave a command:

"Lady Intelligence is right; bring the ambassadors. The beautiful letter of apology that Lady Intelligence will write should be delivered."

While Rehnüma was going to the living room to pick up the telephone, Yağmur began to think about how many things he had learned from this single event:

"How interesting! Even the mind doesn't fully hear what I say. Of course, when delivering it to the ego it does not explain it exactly as I said, but in the way the ego wants to hear. Listening to no one but the devils until now, the ego is listening to the mind and believes it. In fact, it even acts according to what it says. This means that the most powerful creature in this key point is the mind. Convincing the mind means convincing the ego. For it finds a way to deceive the ego. Actually Sir Intelligence is even more influential than Azazel said. Today Dasim also appeared before us. It is an enemy military unit specially trained on the subject of creating conflict among family members. Its whole purpose is to pursue political games that pit allied countries against one another. I have to learn more about this later on. We overcame today's difficulty fairly easily, but Dasim and those Servant has not yet mentioned will not remain idle. In fact, who knows what calculations they are making even at this moment. While they are working this hard, is it time to sleep?"

Rehnüma's voice could be heard from the living room:

"OK, Mom! I apologize again... Forgive me! OK, I'll tell him; he sends his greetings to you, too. Good night to you, too, Mom."

# And Before You: Zalambar

Less than a week had passed since Yağmur had met Servant, but it seemed like he had lived more than he had lived previously in his lifetime. Now not just every day, but every hour had a different meaning. In fact, even every second. In that tiny moment of time, there was so much going on in a person's heart palace.

While thinking about these things as he was going to work on Monday morning, Yağmur also realized that he was not giving much attention to his work. Saying, "Today I'll put things together with some hard work," he felt a little more relaxed. When he arrived at the office and sat down at his desk, the first things that attracted his attention were the company invoices that had come on the same day as Servant's birthday message. They stayed there just as they had been left. It was obvious where he had to start to work.

He was entering the monthly expenditure invoices in order into the accounting program when he noticed the sudden increase in the electric, water and telephone bills. There was an astounding increase of almost 2.5 times over the previous months. He immediately looked at the previous month's production program and the work tables, but he didn't find anything to explain the increases on the invoices. He wanted to go to the factory's production division and understand what was going on.

Because the main activity of the company was production, the only reason for too much expenditure must be what is happening in this four thousand square meters space. In addition to this space there were also administrative offices and workers, but they comprised only one-tenth of it.

When passing by the toilets just across from the workers' dressing rooms, Yağmur heard the sound of water. When he stuck his head into the door of the toilet, he was amazed to see that all the lights and water taps were open. After closing them all, he also turned off the lights in the dressing rooms. Passing through the corridor, the lights burning everywhere caught his attention. These could not have been accidentally left on. It was obvious that something was going on. When he passed through the inner door and entered the machine park, he heard an unbearable noise. All of the machines were running idly. Now it was time to learn what was happening. His attention was caught by a worker who finished his job and should have turned his machine off, but didn't. Saying, "Let's see what is happening. Now I'll understand. *La ilaha illallah. Muhammadu'r-Rasulullah,*" Yağmur suddenly closed his eyes.

The only difference between the palace he was in and his wife's palace was that here the actors were constantly arguing. Playing roles in different TV series, these artists were giving advice to the grand vizier according to their own knowledge:

"Look Sir Vizier! I supported this Zalambar, whoever it is, a lot. In our world this is the law. A young man says, 'Rights are not given, they are taken,' and if necessary he takes his right at gun point. You watched me this much; didn't you learn anything? Also Sir Conscience's complaining like a child drives me crazy. Either you shut him up or I know what to do."

He showed the cover of one of the guns at his waist. The other stouter one was thinking differently:

"Give me a break and listen to me old man! You cannot trust anyone in this world, not even your own father. There's no such thing as five burgers for three cents. You have to be your own man in this world. You shouldn't let anyone take your rights. You have to hit and shoot. That's it."

After these words, the air really heated up. Sir Conscience was continuing to speak helplessly:

"Sir Ego, how many times do I have to say the same things? There is a business contract you made with our ally 'Sir Boss.' He will give us raw material and we will make the manufactured product and give it back. This agreement which has continued this many years without a problem is not destroyed just because we didn't get all that was owed to us last month. Also, let's say we are owed money, what do we gain by misusing the raw materials like water and electricity that he gave? Just as our receivable remains, we also have given harm to Sultan Boss. Let's forego this. Sir

Intelligence will find a way to ask for our receivable anyway."

But Sir Ego didn't agree:

"You stop these criticisms and allow Sir Intelligence to think about how we can give more harm and get our due. If you take into account the news from "Zalambar," Esteemed Boss has already begun to complain. He deserves it! We'll make him regret that he took our right... 'Rights are taken, not given!' That's it!"

Yağmur was very curious about what had happened. Servant came to his rescue:

"All of what you have seen is the work of Zalambar. It is another unit of the Army of Evil. Later on you will learn all the details about this division and how to struggle against them. However, let me briefly mention them. Their purpose is to enter business life and, inciting people against one another, to make them oppress each other. Their slogan is: 'Rights are taken, not given.' Even if they add just one *haram*[7] to ninety-nine *halal*[8] things, they think they have profited. They are expert at showing people something that is not a right to be a right. Even worse, even if someone has not gotten his true right, then they show him illegal means to get it. Just like the situation of the workers in the factory. What is the benefit to them of all this electricity and water they have wasted? Absolute-

7 Religiously forbidden or unlawful.

8 Religiously permited or lawful.

ly zero. However, Zalambar has fooled them so much that they feel relieved. They didn't think at all about the legitimacy of what they did. Don't let this matter go! Let's see who else Zalambar fooled. In addition, as a Servant you have to help this person."

Having explained these, Servant stepped aside.

Yağmur began to think quickly about what he could do. He remembered how he had convinced Lady Intelligence to help Rehnüma yesterday. Now he could try the same thing. He immediately opened his eyes and called out to the foreman:

"How are things going, foreman?"

"Pardon? I can't hear you," the foreman said.

"It's because of the noise from the machines. If your work is finished, turn them off and let's talk a little," Yağmur shouted.

While the frowning foreman extended his hand to the off switch, he didn't neglect to take a side glance at the Accounting Department Manager. What had brought them to this point of rebellion? When the machine became silent, Yağmur continued:

"I see that the lights, water and machines have been left on for no reason. The bills that came this month are much larger than the previous ones. Will you tell me what you want to do by this?"

A "Zalambar" gleam of light formed in the foreman's eyes from joy. Then he spoke cheerfully as one whose goal had been reached:

"Shouldn't you know this best? Did you think that we would do nothing when you seized our work last month? On the one hand, you force us to work and, on the other hand, you don't pay us. Well, they didn't say, 'Rights are taken, not given!" for nothing. We're taking our rights."

Yağmur stopped a moment in view of what he heard. He thought, "This is not possible!" But it was obvious from the foreman's behavior, which required courage and being in the right, that he was not lying. Tayfun followed up the work hours and payment job. In order to learn the truth, he needed to leave immediately, but he had a few words for Sir Intelligence whom he believed could convince the foreman:

"Look, my dear foreman! If there is an injustice, you can be sure that I will remedy this in the shortest possible time. However, as for the saying, 'Rights are taken, not given,' I don't agree with this. If you think like this, you will begin to see everything as permissible. You don't need to wait for it to be given to you; since its your right, then you will take it! But what if it isn't your right? What if there is something to it that you don't know about? But let's say it really is your right like the work that you have done. Then what needs to be done is to use legitimate means. The accounting department could have made a mistake, or the administrative department could have made a wrong decision, or perhaps payment was not made due to a passing problem. Just as what you are doing now does not benefit you at all, in the end it can get you into trouble."

"What do you mean? Are you threatening me?"

"No, of course not. The electricity and water that has been wasted will for certain return to you and your family as a problem one day. The drought that can occur in hot weather after this winter, which saw very little rain, will make us look for every drop of water that you have wasted. Wasted electricity that is not turned into production is the same. As the current electricity decreases, the remaining amount will become more valuable. Of course, you will see this value in the bills that come to your house and that you have difficulty paying every month. Think about it now: You don't get your rights with the electricity and water you have wasted and, at the same time, you have to pay for all this together with your loved ones. Come and abandon this. And I will examine the reason for your trouble with your pay. Come on, foreman, and have a good day!"

Sir Intelligence was listening to what was said very carefully! Great minds think alike. Clearly understanding what was being said, Sir Intelligence's essential task now was to explain all this in a way that Sir Ego could understand it. That's what he did:

"Look, Sir Ego! I was really impressed by what this guy said! He spoke truthfully. If you continue like this, eventually we will have to give a product in return for the raw materials we used. If there is no product, then we'll have to pay for their value. In other words, in every case we will lose. Come and I'll find a way for you to ask for our rights, OK?"

"Do whatever you want! Everyone is talking! Enough! Shut up! Look at me! Yes, I am talking to you both. Bolat Manidar and Yusuf Kıroğlu. This is enough. You've turned this place into a bear garden!"

# Kamir and Miswat Partnership

Due to Sir Intelligence, Yağmur had again hit the target. He understood that the most effective way to convince people was to address their intelligence. If he had not done this, but had directly targeted the foreman's ego and criticized him saying, "What do you think you are doing? You call this work? Where's the logic of this?", Sir Ego would surely have rejected these, not thought for a minute about what he was doing, and not accepted his mistake.

Now it was Tayfun's turn. A number of scenarios had begun to form in Yağmur's head, and the worst of these was the possibility that the workers' pay had been embezzled. However, it was impossible to think that such a thing would not be noticed. Then how could a person attempt such a thing knowing it would come out? As a sultan, he went to his office consulting Sir Intelligence. He went to his desk without letting anyone know what was going on. He thought that the lunch break would be the best time to talk with Tayfun. Meanwhile the accumulated work would be lightened up.

Five minutes before the lunch break Tayfun was getting ready to go. Because Yağmur couldn't say anything in front of the others, he followed him outside. But by the time he reached the parking lot, Tayfun had long since driven away. Getting caught up by this sudden development, Yağmur got into his car and began to follow him.

After a little while they stopped at a betting booth. With a roll of money he took out of his pocket, Tayfun extended a stack of coupons to the man. Then he took something resembling a receipt, quickly returned to his car and continued on his way. Of course, Yağmur was following him. After they entered the center of the city, they began to advance along side streets. Coming to these isolated places for the first time, Yağmur was a little apprehensive. If he was not curious about what Tayfun was doing in such a place, he would have long since turned back. But when he saw him park his car, Yağmur immediately pulled off to the side and followed him.

They entered a dilapidated office building in front of which a crowd had assembled. Full of cigarette stubs stuck to phlegm, the stairs lead to a secluded shop with windows covered over with newspapers.

The man who allowed Tayfun in first searched him and then asked him something. Yağmur carefully went up the steps to face this question he didn't know the answer to. For not falling on these disgusting steps was not easy. The enormous man at the door searched him and then asked:

"Paper or bones?"

He would learn later that this was a categorization of games played with cards and dice, but at that moment he was only able to say, “Paper, please,” not knowing what was customary.

When the word “please” was about to mess everything up, he saved the situation by saying in a deep voice, “BROTHER.”

“Then downstairs,” he said, showing the stairway inside. The good side was that he had seen Tayfun going downstairs as he put his head in the door.

This place didn’t resemble the outside of the building at all. The floors were completely covered with red carpeting, the columns were covered with golden brass, some spaces were full of tables with four chairs, some were filled with people in rows, their eyes fixated on the paper in front of them, listening to the bingo numbers. Tayfun had joined these. Afraid of being recognized, Yağmur immediately went outside and, getting into his car, he returned to work. For he had seen as much as he needed to see, even if it saddened him.

Tayfun returned a little after the lunch break. Meanwhile, Yağmur had prepared well what he was going to say. Again he would explain things to Sir Intelligence and he would convince Sir Ego. In addition, he would embolden Sir Conscience in order for Tayfun to be able to admit what he had done.

He had planned everything so well that in order for Tayfun not to be embarrassed in front of his friends, he had left a note on his desk, "Follow me out of the room. We need to talk." When Yağmur said, "Selma, I have a little job to do outside, but I'll return in half an hour," Tayfun immediately followed.

They sat down in the pavilion in the factory's garden. Tayfun was an intelligent person. Without saying anything, he waited for Yağmur to begin. Because he wanted to understand the current situation, Yağmur closed his eyes and pronounced the tawhid internally. But something totally unexpected happened: He found himself at the door of the palace, not in the palace. At first he didn't understand, but when he saw that there was no writing on the door, he realized the truth that would make him very sad: Tayfun had long since lost his throne.

Suddenly Servant appeared and began to explain the situation:

"Isn't this a situation you haven't yet seen in the palaces you visited? It is apparent that

'Kamir' has grabbed Tayfun's throne."

"Who is Kamir?"

"It is another unit in Azazel's army. It got its name from the devils comprising this division. The Kamir's only job is to put before people every kind of gambling in order to drive them to "Gambling Mountain." I say every kind because the Kamirs, like other units of the Army of Evil, try and develop new weapons everyday. For this reason, right now there are so many weapons called games instead of gambling that if people are able to escape from one, they fall into traps with the others."

"You're right. For example, everyone was playing bingo in the place I went today. I'm sure that most of them did not think they were gambling. I remember very well that in my childhood we also would sit down with relatives and play bingo. However tiny amounts were put in our hands as school allowance, still it was always called a game. An understanding of playing that began so innocently turns into a huge danger later on; I saw today with my own eyes how it leads a person to stealing."

"Come and let's have a look inside. You remember the verse in the chapter Ya-Sin, don't you?"

"Yes! It's very short, so I memorized it."

"Great! Recite it and let's go in," said Servant. They both became invisible and entered the palace.

This place did not resemble his own palace at all. After they passed through the door, a long, straight corridor took them directly to the grand hall. Everyplace was dirty and a heavy odor had enveloped every side. Yağmur thought for a moment that he remembered this odor. He was not accustomed to it, but he recognized it. When he saw the guard at the hall's door, his memory immediately answered: this odor was the smell of the gambling hall he had gone to today. "I guess if this bouncer could see us, he would again ask, 'Paper or bones?'" he thought. When they entered the hall, this foul odor had become unbearable.

The reason for all this was there sitting on the throne that did not belong to him, but which he had usurped.

Yağmur looked around to see who was managing things. Sir Ego was standing at attention just next to Kamir. There was no trace of Sir Conscience. He felt a little better when he saw Sir Intelligence, but when he found that he was "studying" the pile of numerical, wager coupons, his positive feeling didn't last long. The rest of the hall was filled with players who never left their tables and who were holding on to the cards and dice as if they were the source of life.

As for Kamir, he occasionally got up from the throne and, going to the side of a player whose chain seemed to be loosening a little, he would get upset. Then he would politely pat him on the head and say:

"Don't be upset; continue! I am here to serve you. I wish you abundant devils," and then he would return to his throne.

Just then a familiar face came through the door. It was no other than the indispensable messenger of every palace, Waswas. Clearly upset, this miserable creature began to speak breathlessly:

"Honorable Kamir, the news is very bad, sir. It has been understood that we have not given the money we owe to the workers necessitated by the work agreement we made with Esteemed Boss before. The ambassador of our ally Honorable Yağmur who was assigned to look into the matter is about to arrive at our palace. You have to immediately think of a solution, sir."

Kamir replied in an extremely calm and even brazen way:

"What am I going to think, you miserable creature? Let Sir Intelligence do the thinking."

But Sir Intelligence was unaware of what was happening and still busy with the coupons in front of him. Raising his voice a little more, Kamir said:

"I'm talking to you, Sir Intelligence. Look, they're coming to ask for an account of the money we lost because of you. Drop this work that you can't manage and think of a solution." Sir Intelligence looked vacantly for a long time at Kamir's face. Just like Tayfun had stared stupidly at Yağmur's face. At that time Yağmur had thought to himself, "So this silence is because he hasn't thought of anything."

Then Kamir angrily broke the silence:

"You'll see what happens! When Sultan Yağmur's ambassador comes, you'll see what I do to you when you don't talk like this!"

Yağmur was going to leave the palace when something caught his attention and he silently whispered in Servant's ear: "I don't see Sir Conscience. If he were here maybe he could have taken some precautions before things got this much out of hand. Where is he?"

"The first thing that a devil from the Army of Evil will do if he is going to sit on the throne is to imprison Sir Conscience. As long as he lives there is always a chance that he can get out, but there are so many who do not... One of our duties as Servant is to rescue Sir Conscience in this kind of a situation and take him to Master Spirit. If this can be done, it is possible that the throne can be returned to its rightful owner. But this job is harder than you think and you are not yet prepared for this," Servant said.

Surprised, Yağmur replied:

"What do you mean, I'm not ready? You have taught me so many things that I feel I am ready for everything."

Servant's response was very thought-provoking:

"Do you know what we call a Servant whose time has not yet come? 'Servant of defeat.' In other words, you're not fully a Servant yet. Just as there are things you can do, there are also things you can't do. You need to be a little more patient. Don't worry, you will understand what I wanted to say soon."

After this one moment of keeping his eyes closed, Yağmur began speaking:

"Look, sir. I don't want to mislead you with the questions I'm going to ask. The best thing would be for you to tell me what you know about last month's payment of wages to the workers. I'm listening."

It was such a good opening that Tayfun's Sir Intelligence, who was waiting for the questions, paused for a moment and, not having an opportunity to make up a story, intended to tell the true story.

But something unexpected happened. Feeling something strange, Yağmur entered the palace. Again Waswas had come breathlessly and was saying something hastily to Kamir:

"Sir, as you ordered, I went to Esteemed Miswat without losing any time and got a written copy of all he said. Shall I read it?"

"It's not necessary. Let's not lose time. Later we'll attract suspicion. Immediately give this to Honorable Yağmur's ambassador and let him take it," Kamir said and took what Sir Intelligence had prepared, gave the letter from Miswat instead, and sent off the ambassador.

Yağmur needed to arrive before the ambassador, but again his curiosity prevented this and he quickly asked Servant who was standing beside him:

"Where did this Miswat come from?"

"It's another division of the Army of Evil. The most intelligent devils are chosen for this unit. Their whole job is to lie. Both devils and ambassadors of Sir Ego constantly come to this headquarters and take lies and scenarios regarding different situations from here. As soon as you left, that's what Kamir did and he will respond to you with a lie coming from Miswat. He hurried because remaining without a response for a time would cause suspicion. You would understand that he was lying. If you hadn't seen what was happening here, I'm sure you would have believed Miswat's letter."

"It would be a good idea for you to come back," Servant said.

While Yağmur opened his eyes, Tayfun had already begun to speak:

"Look, sir, I'm not going to explain all my problems here and make you feel sorry for me. However, I would like you to know that last year my mother underwent a very serious operation. The doctors saw no other hope for her to live, so it was that important. Think a moment, without the operation I was going to lose my only Valide Sultan. I got bank credit for this operation which was as expensive as it was important. Then when I couldn't pay it back, I borrowed money from a loan shark. Now the mafia are pressuring me. My life is going to be the blood money for my mother's life. I have thought of every means of paying them my debt. Finally I helplessly tied my hope to games of chance. To tell the truth, I just took the workers' pay as a trust; I was going to give it to them in a few days. But things didn't go as I had thought they would. If you noticed, I wasn't even at lunch today. I am trying and will try to make up for this mistake. Please, give me a little time, please."

Yağmur was extremely affected by what he had heard. Just as Servant had said, if you didn't know the facts, it would be very easy to believe it. In fact, he could have taken all the money in his pocket and given it to Tayfun. But he knew that all this was a lie. In addition, he was aware that there would be no use in speaking to a palace where Sir Conscience wasn't even present. He could only say:

"OK, I'll try and handle the situation a little longer."

Yağmur realized very clearly that Servant was right and that he was not yet able to handle every situation.

That evening while returning home, again his head was full of questions:

"Dasim, Zalambar, Kamir, Miswat... Who knows how many more divisions there were in the Army of Evil. Well, when am I going to learn how to fight with them and how to rescue innocent people from their hands? Servant says I'm not ready. OK, maybe he's right, but if things continue like this I'll never be ready. What do I have to my credit except for memorizing the devils' names and duties? When am I going to become a full Servant? I wish there were a shorter road to this."

Having said this, he was unaware of what awaited him in the near future.

# Great Danger: Awar

While days were flying by, Yağmur's education regarding the kinds of devils and their duties was continuing. During this process he learned about "Sabar." The duty of this evil division was to approach people during times of difficulty and encourage them to rebel. It was their duty to prevent people from thinking that the difficulty had been sent by God as a trial and to encourage them to rebel and say, "Was I going to see this, too?"; "Bad things always happen to me!"; and "To Hell with this world and my dreams."

Then he learned about "Hinzap" and Walhan." They are the Prayer and ablution devils. Their duty is to make people stray from their path with unimaginable tricks and deceptions so that people will avoid ablution and Prayer or, if they perform them, to do it erroneously and then to neglect them completely.

In addition, he learned about "Khumar the Master of Intoxication." This vile creature was the owner of alcohol glasses which people saw as a means of forgetting about their problems rather than solving them. It was the task of this unit to put chains around people's necks and take them to drinking tables and then to leave them chained there alone with their problems.

Also there are the "Awar" but Yağmur had not yet met them. He had not met them because he didn't even know they exist. If only he had never known...

One evening when he got into his car in the company parking lot, he was startled by someone tapping on the window. It was the general manager's secretary, Arzu. She called to him in a soft tone:

"Sir, can I ask a favor from you?"

"Of course, what is it?"

"There's a matter I wanted to talk with you about. If you can give me a little time, I would be very pleased," she said and, without waiting for an answer, she walked around the car and sat down in the front seat.

With a little shy and shaky voice, Yağmur was able to say:

"Please go ahead, I'm listening."

Gaining courage from Yağmur's shaky voice, Arzu said:

"Not here. It's the end of the workday. Someone might see us. I know of a nice place. We can have a something to eat and talk at the same time."

She hadn't left time for Yağmur to think. Although it cannot be said that even if he had a chance, Yağmur, who had been swept up by the speed and attractiveness of the event, would have been able to think.

After a long dinner, they got into the car to take Arzu home. After a ride of about twenty minutes, they arrived in front of her house. Until that time indirectly showing her intention with suggestive words, Arzu acted quickly and displayed a sudden closeness. While being relieved by attaining something she had wanted for a long time, to the contrary, Yağmur became uncomfortable because he had missed something he had wanted for a long time. It was as if he had woken up from the spell he had fallen into when Arzu got into his car and, coming to his senses, he became aware of the disgraceful situation he had fallen into. Hastily he said:

"I have to go."

Arzu got out of the car, but before she understood what was happening, he had left.

Even though he opened the car window and loosened his tie, he was unable to breathe comfortably. While the fire of regret that had begun to burn inside of him became stronger, Yağmur thought that the only way to put out this fire was to die. He had come to such a condition that he didn't want to live; he couldn't even raise his head from shame and look at the road. If he looked, he couldn't see anything because of his tears. He was going, but he didn't know where he went or would go. Yağmur had let go of himself... He wasn't trying to breathe... He didn't care where he went... He wasn't curious about where death would come from... He was just waiting...

He didn't know how long he had been driving like that, but when the car stopped with a loud noise, shaking, he realized he had struck something. When he got out of the car to see what had happened, he was still crying. The Servant ring he had seen on his finger while holding the steering wheel had inflamed the fire inside of him so much that it was not possible to extinguish it. There didn't appear to be too much damage. But although he tried again and again to start the car, which had run onto the sidewalk on his right and struck a tree, he was not successful. The interesting thing was that the branches of the tree he had struck extended to the cemetery wall.

He didn't know how he had come here, but he knew very well where he would go. As Servant's words came to his mind, he quickened his steps. As if he had known this would happen, he had said "Servant of defeat." Wasn't what he had just lived a full defeat? Had Servant meant this when he said, "Don't worry, you'll understand shortly what I meant to say"?

While jumping over the cemetery wall at night, he saw before his eyes his coming about a week or ten days before for a rescue operation and what he had lived after that. Everything he remembered made him even sadder and became fuel for the fire inside of him. Had Sultan Yağmur, whom they had saved with all the trouble and self-sacrifice of Servant, now become the captive of a woman? He grieved deeply when he thought about how he would be able to look Servant in the face. He took off the ring which he didn't feel he deserved and held it tightly in his hands.

When he reached his grave, he threw himself on it and began to cry as hard as he could...

He calmed down a little; there were no more tears left to shed. A hand touching his shoulder brought him to his senses:

"Do you know why your grandfather named you Yağmur?"

"So people can die from the drought while they are waiting for mercy from me?"

"No, just as rain is a vehicle for mercy to people, you also can be a vehicle for mercy so people can be saved."

Yes, their first meeting that took place about two weeks ago was being repeated. When Yağmur had asked at their first meeting, "Who are you?" Servant had said, "I am Servant, just like you." This had reminded Yağmur of an event his grandfather had spoken about:

"Yunus Emre had spent days far from the dervish lodge. When he felt regret and returned, he put his head on the threshold of his master's door and waited to be forgiven. When the wife of his master, the noble Taptuk, saw Yunus at the door, she felt very sorry for him and wanted to help him. She said: 'Now I am going to bring Hodja Effendi. He is very old and can't see well. When he goes through the door he will ask, 'Who are you?' You say, 'Yunus.' If Hodja Effendi asks, 'Which Yunus? Our Yunus?' then know that he has forgiven you. But if he only asks, 'Which Yunus?' then know that he is still offended.'"

This was a good opportunity to understand whether or not there had been a change in Servant's affection:

"Who are you?"

"I am Servant just like you."

Becoming a little relieved by this answer, Yağmur stood up and turning his head towards Servant, said:

"Please forgive me but I'm not going to be able to do this work. How can I help others when I can't yet help myself? Excuse me and please give this sacred ring to someone who deserves it."

He extended the ring in his hand. With that deep smile and calmness, Servant took the ring and then put it on Yağmur's finger again.

"Don't make a hasty decision. Come and let's sit down. Listen well to what I'm going to say," Servant said.

He took Yağmur by the arm and they sat down at the edge of the cemetery. Then he began to explain:

"You remember where our journey began, don't you? We saw together Azazel's enmity towards Adam and his victory in their first struggle. After this defeat of Adam's we don't see a second one. Why do you think we don't?"

"I have no idea."

"OK, then let me explain in terms you can understand. There is something called a hierarchy of needs. In other words, without meeting certain of their needs, people are not aware of their next needs. For example, think of a man: if he is left naked on the top of a mountain, what will he need first?"

"Something to wear, of course."

"That's right! Let's say that after a long search he meets this need. What next?"

"He'll probably want to fill his stomach."

"Absolutely! He will want to meet his need for water and food. After that he will want to find shelter. Then the hierarchy of needs continues in this shape. After one need is met, he begins to feel a new need. In your opinion, would a man in this situation think of pleasure and comfort instead of finding something to wear or looking for something to eat?"

"I don't think so!"

"Adam was punished like this after his first mistake. His celestial clothing was taken and he was put on the top of a mountain in this world. If you notice, actually this is not a punishment. It was an aid for him to turn to his basic needs and not be fooled by the trickery of the devil. In this situation Adam only focused on his immediate needs. The situation he was in was so difficult that he had no time, strength or opportunity for the pleasure, entertainment and comfort that the devil invited him to."

"Actually these are perfect points. Once I was also without any money. I was a student at a university far from my hometown and I even had to walk to the examination.

When I returned home extremely tired, I thought: When I didn't have any money in my pocket, nothing called me from outside. I remember that I didn't even leave the house for several days. Of course, I didn't commit any sins. I just filled my stomach with the pulses on hand, and I was grateful because I didn't have anything more."

"There is something more here and it relates to you closely. Adam was removed from among the many blessings that he had not done anything to get, and, with the condition of living his whole life truthfully, he was promised these things again. Generally the situation of people from their creation is like this. However much effort you make to attain something, you give it that much value when you get it. The same thing is true for you. Think of the spiritual blessings you have received since we met. Whenever you want you can enter your own or someone else's inner world. You not only see but recognize by name and duty the enemies that others cannot even see. But these blessings that were given to you without your effort have now been taken from you. A devil you had not yet met named Awar deceived you. Assigned the duty of showing fornication among people to be good and pulling them into this swamp, this unit of the Army of Evil caught you off guard at an unexpected moment. At a moment when you were not on the throne, Grand Vizier Sir Ego and Commander Lust rebelled against you with instructions from Awar. They bound you—Sultan Yağmur—with chains. They also taped the mouths of Sir Conscience and Sir Intelligence. And there was no one else to protect you."

"What you say is very true. Throughout those moments it was as if my mind was not in my head, as if I was in a dream. Without understanding what happened, I lived everything like a sultan who is not ruling."

"As I said, especially as a sultan, an armed power is necessary to protect you against Sir Ego, Commander Lust and Commander Anger. Even in the external world things work like this. Someone with a gun in his hand can make a raid, make threats and force others to do what he says. But just think that you have formed a special and powerful team that will protect you from them and make them obey you."

"How can that be?"

"Can there be gain without pain, Yağmur? The way to get all those blessings that were bestowed upon you from the beginning and more is for you to struggle like Adam. In order for you to establish and train this special team, you need 'forty days' that will pass with difficulty, hunger, thirst and weariness. In other words, forty days of penitence."

"Where will this forty days take place? How would it be possible? I have work and a family."

"Don't worry! I have taken care of everything. What is important is for you to want it. This forty days will take place in a space where you will not go up more than the first steps of the hierarchy of needs, like in a cave."

"If there is no other road to becoming a Servant like you, then I want to do it. However, with the condition that you are at my side."

"Unfortunately this is not possible, Yağmur. There you will face all your fears, your realities and you biggest enemy. You will die in that cave and then be born to this world again. If permission comes from the Holy Sphere, I will try to visit you from time to time. Don't worry!"

"Only my car doesn't work. How will we go?"

"I've arranged that, too. Let's walk to the gate."

When they came to the door, Yağmur was not surprised to see that it was open. He had become so accustomed to strange things during the time that he had spent with Servant, that very few things in this life could surprise him. If we exclude Awar, maybe nothing...

A running car was waiting for them on the side of the road. Yağmur knew the owner of this extremely luxurious and ostentatious car, because he knew the car. He had seen it in a special place everyday in the parking lot. It was his boss, Adil's car. In fact, when looking a little closer... yes, he was at the wheel. There was no end to Servant's surprises.

Servant opened a back door of the car for Yağmur. After he got in, Servant sat in the front. With a joking tone he asked Yağmur:

"Do you know Adil?"

"What do you mean? Of course, I know him. He's my boss."

"I wouldn't use the word 'know' for this little information about him. He is also a very good Servant and a close friend of your grandfather's," Servant said.

Yağmur noticed the ring on Âdil's finger. He realized that he had not looked carefully before at this ring which he had seen several times. It was just like the ring on his finger, with one small difference. There was a symbol on both edges of the ring. Although he couldn't see too well in the dark, it was a symbol like a "No U-turn" sign. Although he was very curious, due to his respect and shyness he wasn't able to ask the meaning of it. To confirm Servant's words, Adil began to speak:

"Due to my young age, I think I need to explain my friendship with your grandfather. May God approve of him, I met that blessed man when I was still in high school. I had fallen into a swamp at a young age. While waiting for a hand to save me and a breath to give me life, he found me. He introduced me to a group of friends my age and he always called me 'Friend' until he died. From that day forward I tried my best to be worthy of his compliment. God willing, I'll continue until I die..."

Servant interrupted with a question:

"By the way, you remember the road, don't you?"

"How can I forget? I will always remember this road I followed to kill the sinner Adil and be resurrected with my will. And this ring that you gave me later on. A symbol of loyalty to one's oath, this ring always reminded me of that cave in my most difficult times and in situations when

I was at my weakest. The promise you took from me when you put the ring on my finger was never forgotten. Now I am curious. There was an old ring you took back that day; what did you do with it?"

"It is on the finger of its temporary owner, waiting to be exchanged for a new one..."

# A Grave or a Womb?

*"Die before you die!"*

They stopped on a path outside the city. The car couldn't proceed any further. When they got out of the car, Yağmur shyly mentioned his concern:

"What about Rehnüma? What will happen to her?"

"Don't worry! Adil and his wife went and explained the situation to her. Of course, not all the details. Don't be concerned. She is going to spend the next forty days in her father's house. She sent some things she prepared for you," Servant said and extended a middle-sized bag.

When his wife came to his mind, he remembered his mistake of last evening and his eyes filled with tears. Meanwhile Servant asked Adil to wait at the car and he and Yağmur embraced and said good-bye:

"Don't worry, Yağmur, everything is going to be very beautiful for you. Maybe now is not the appropriate time, but I thought it would make you more comfortable to know that the workers have been paid. After he talked with you, Tayfun came to see me. 'My conscience does not leave me alone,'" he said.

At that moment Yağmur was looking at the sparkle in Servant's eyes. It was obvious that today there was another rescue operation...

Servant and Yağmur began to walk up the rocky path from the skirts of the mountain. Needing to explain everything necessary before reaching the cave, Servant immediately began to speak:

"When we made the journey to your heart, we saw five rivers emptying into the lake behind the palace; do you remember?"

"Yes, in fact, I watched them for a long time the first night I stayed there."

"Actually everything ends there. All the organs in your body and all the forces in your inner world like Sir Ego, Commander Lust and Commander Anger are nourished from these rivers. If they are nurtured purely, they will be obedient, but if they are nourished with dirty things, they will be rebellious. The things that you see with your eyes, hear with your ears, do with your hands and feet, say with your tongue and send to your stomach should always be clean. If you recall, I mentioned setting up a Repentance Filtering Facility in order to clean the water currently accumulated in the lake. But if while you clean the lake, on the one hand, you carry dirty water to the rivers, on the other hand, all your efforts will be in vain. During this forty days of penitence we are going to shut off all the water coming from the rivers. Just as this forty days is sufficient to clean the water in the lake, it will be enough for us to set up a

'Special Team of Will' to provide for only pure water to come from the rivers later on."

"How am I going to form this special team?"

"By not eating, drinking, sleeping, speaking, seeing and hearing. In other words, by opposing all the wishes and desires of Sir Ego. By accepting that he is just a vizier and that you are the sultan who will command him. Forty days is a sufficient period of time to make a habit in both a person's inner world and external world. If you can make him accustomed to obeying you during this period, this habit will continue throughout the remainder of your life. A person who makes his ego bow down can fight with the whole Army of Evil."

"OK, but how can I live without eating?"

"It's not quite like that! You can eat enough to stay alive. Consequently, you're going to eat, drink and sleep just to meet your needs, not for the sake of your ego's desires. This opposition that you will show on every front will enable you to prove your own strength and power, while forming your 'Special Team of Will,' to all your armies, especially Commander Lust and Commander Anger. When they see this self-confidence, they will obey you. At any rate, you are going to choose the soldiers for the special team from them."

"So the secret is to eat little."

"Absolutely! Remember the hierarchy of needs. After a person follows lust for food, it is followed by sexual lust. A person who has overcome these two lusts will turn towards possessing a house and goods. It is not in vain that people say, 'When two hearts are one, there is love in a cottage." Until someone possesses some goods, he falls into arguments and jealousy of others. Then a person who becomes puffed up due to the things he owns and likes himself will look at things he doesn't own and feel envy and hostility. Then he begins to oppress others in order to possess those things. And believe me, Yağmur, there is no end to this. Even he who owns the whole world, he will look at others who are breathing and say, 'You are consuming my oxygen,' and he will continue to oppress."

"What you say is true. It seems very logical to me."

"That's not all. Can a person who is hungry and thirsty sleep?"

"I don't think so! It happened to me once and I wandered around the streets until morning."

"Sleeping little is tied to eating little. Remember when you fasted. Although people who fast today have full stomachs.... When you are hungry, your interest in the opposite sex decreases. You are more interested in food. Even if a person says something negative to you, you will hear the growling in your stomach rather than that person. Moreover, you won't have the energy to oppress others. Actually this is the wisdom in fasting, but people do not realize this. Even at the sahur (meal before sunrise) table people warn one another, 'Eat this, too, or you will be hungry tomorrow,' and 'Don't eat this or you will be thirsty tomorrow.'"

"If this is what I have to do for forty days, it's easy."

"Wait a minute. If it were that simple, everyone would do it. Or our religion would command everyone to do it. Throughout this forty days Azazel and his soldiers will attack you in unimaginable ways. Your greatest fears will appear before you. Azazel and his accomplices will try and turn you back from this sacred path which is a salvation from your ego. You are going to struggle with them alone. There is no door to the cave. You can leave when you want. The only power that can hold you there is your love for God and your desire for servanthood to Him. You will spend all your time here with worship, *dhikr*,[9] Prayer and repentance. You will eat your food consisting only of seven bites and three swallows of water everyday after you have performed the Evening Prayer. When I occasionally bring you food, I will ask about your condition if permission is given. Now put the things I explained to you aside and start living them. When we first met I told you, 'You will learn everything by living it'; this is true for these, too. You have to obtain the benefits of hunger, thirst, sleeplessness, not seeing anyone, not hearing anyone and not speaking with anyone by means of living these. Otherwise, knowing, listening and saying, 'Very logical and very nice!' is of no use."

"I understand. God willing, I am going to do this. Please pray for me."

---

[9] Recitation of one or some of God's Names.

"The prayers of all the Servants are with you. Always try and feel that they are with you. Don't forget, they all believe in you!"

These last words greatly affected Yağmur. He was an individual from the Group of Servants and all Servants trusted in him. He could not disappoint them.

## Day 1

Everything appeared to be going well. His stomach growled a little around noontime, but it wasn't that important. The cave's being a little cold helped from the angle of preventing sleepiness.

The time came for breaking his fast which he had strongly anticipated. He joyfully and excitedly opened the bag of provisions, but was disappointed. There was only bread and water there. As Servant had said, he ate only seven bites of bread. Then he drank three sips of water and was astonished. He was not full yet. His hunger only diminished a little, that's all. He was aware that if he ate the rest of the bread, he still would not be full. In addition, he thought he should act cautiously because he didn't know when Servant would bring more food.

## Day 2

He was a little tired, but he was very hungry. He had only been able to sleep four hours during the night. While the cave became cold yesterday and helped his hunger and prevented his sleep, today his hunger helped the cold to make him shiver.

He had prayed approximately enough compensation Prayer for fifty days and his knees hurt a lot. In addition, his isolation had made him feel a little lonely.

## Day 4

He had eaten a little more than seven bites during the past two days and he had nothing left to eat. He thought about leaving the cave to look for something to eat, but it occurred to him that this was just something contrived by his ego. In addition, Servant could not have abandoned him to death here. He could not be an orphan as he had thought for four days. But he was alone and there was no one else. This situation drew him much closer to God. Today he was praying a lot more than in the previous days. In fact, at the time to break his fast he could only pray.

## Day 5

His not being able to break fast yesterday had left him very feeble. Especially not drinking water was very hard to endure. Suddenly he involuntarily said "water." It was the first time that he had heard his voice for days, but he wasn't certain. This voice had sounded so foreign to him that it seemed as if someone else was talking.

A feeling of alienation towards himself came alive inside of him. He realized that he had never really known himself. Strangely enough, he was afraid of himself. He thought that actually it was not this cave, but himself whom he wanted to abandon. But where could a person escape from himself?

Because he didn't have the strength to perform the Prayer, he thought about these things until evening. There was not much time until the breaking of the fast, but for him there was no fast breaking. Because there was nothing to break the fast with... Together with the setting sun he made a last effort and stood up; he walked towards the entrance to the cave. The question he had asked Servant in the war with Azazel's army came to mind:

"When is God's help going to come?"

Then he thought of Servant and his answer:

"Don't worry. For certain God's help is close."

Yağmur's eyes filled with tears. Then he wept... Who was going to comfort him now?

When he remained alone with himself to whom he felt a complete stranger, who was going to befriend him?

Thinking of friends, his mind turned to Abraham. At the time when he was about to be thrown into the fire and the angels came one-by-one and offered friendship to him, he even rejected Gabriel and said, "My Friend knows my situation very well." He had not taken anyone but God as his friend.

"My Lord! I don't want any other friend but You. In this world where I don't even know myself, I do not know anyone as my friend. You are my friend and You know my situation very well," he said.

Then together with the setting sun, he returned to the darkening cave.

He made a *tayammum*[10] and could only perform the Prayer sitting down. He was so weak that he could not stand up for Servant or even say welcome when Servant entered the cave. Grasping the gravity of the situation, Servant immediately acted and first gave some water to Yağmur to drink. Then he took out the food he had brought. Even though it was cold, there was soup, a few olives and some honey for the meal.

After the meal it seemed that Yağmur had found new life. They still did not say anything. While Servant got ready to leave, he said:

"Is there anything so far that you want to ask me?"

Yağmur thought a little, swallowed a couple of times and then asked a very unexpected question. It was the first time that he had seen Servant laugh this loud:

"Why do we swallow the olive pits?"

Servant's laughter was replaced by his compassionate voice:

"Yağmur! You can even ask this under these circumstances! You are really very unique."

---

[10] Ablution with clean soil, using earth for ritual purity in the absence of water.

This olive pit issue which had been a mystery to Yağmur for years was clarified:

"Since long ago friends of God are very careful on the subject of eating and drinking. They try and suffice with as little as possible. Named in the Quran, the olive became their most indispensable friend on this difficult journey, for olive pits are the last of any food to be digested in the stomach. Consequently, remaining in the stomach between ten and fourteen hours, these pits give a feeling of fullness for a long time to someone who swallows them."

For the first time in days Yağmur saw a friend among the walls which he saw as his enemy. He heard a friendly voice in the silence he knew to be his enemy. He forgot five days of suffering with a few sweet words. While Servant left behind his best memories, Yağmur looked after him for a little while. Easily distinguished in the moonlight with his white clothing, this blessed man seemed to be a hand of friendship extended to him from God.

## Day 10

Hunger, thirst and sleeplessness had put their swords in their sheaths and begun to slowly show their friendly faces. Yağmur was not very worried for the remaining days. In fact, he was almost preferring to remain in this cave over the life outside. He began to perform the Evening Prayer full of gratitude for all these feelings. He recited the chapter Al-Fatiha with deep concentration.

He suddenly froze before what he saw. He couldn't speak, his throat was dry, and he couldn't breathe. That creature, which he feared the most in his life and which he admitted at every opportunity, had curled up on the Prayer mat, raised his head and was waiting: A large, yellow, cold snake!

Yağmur immediately put his left foot behind him. His other foot was about to follow as an ordinary reflex when he paused. Where could he escape? Regardless of where he went in this cave, in the end the snake could catch him. Escaping outside would mean he had broken his promise. In a time short enough to recite the additional portion of the Qur'an, Yağmur had thought of so many things:

"O my Lord! For certain everything moves with Your permission and command. I am here for Your command. I will bow down and prostrate because You commanded it. This creature could not have come here without Your command. And, again, it will not harm me without Your permission. In that case, everything is in Your power and I have surrendered to You.

Again, when Abraham was going to sacrifice his son Ishmael, Your command was fulfilled; the knife hit his neck. But because it didn't have Your permission, it didn't cut.

When another Prophet, Jonah, was thrown into the sea, Your command was fulfilled; that huge fish swallowed Jonah. But because it didn't have Your permission, it couldn't eat him.

Thus, my Lord! I believe that this snake came here with Your command, but it won't bite as long as You don't give permission. Both good and evil are from You."

When Yağmur bowed down, the snake had uncoiled a little and extending its head towards him, it began to show its teeth. Yağmur stood up. He made perhaps the most serious decision of his life. Maybe for the first time he stood up against fear and challenged death. Then he said "*Allahu Akbar*," closed his eyes, held his breath and prostrated at full speed...

## Day 11

When Servant entered the cave, very little time remained until breaking of the fast. After waiting a little, Yağmur couldn't wait any more and he began to describe what had happened the day before. He explained what he thought while he was standing up, what he felt when he was bowing down, his determination when he stood up and how the snake disappeared when he made prostration. When he had finished, he looked curiously as if he were asking a question. Knowing his student very well, Servant knew he was waiting for an answer:

"A Servant who will serve in God's path has to be fearless. For actually the thing called fear is just a trick in your brain. Think of what you fear when you are afraid. For example, what you experienced yesterday: The moment you saw the snake, an event came to life in your mind. You imagined that you made prostration and the snake struck you. In other words, something that has not yet taken place and that may never take place frightens you. It is the same for a person who is afraid of a dog. As soon as he sees the animal, he imagines in his mind that the dog runs towards him, jumps on him with full force and bites him. Meanwhile the mechanism called the subconscious perceives this scenario as real and the hypothalamus sends a signal to the glands above the kidneys to secrete hormones called adrenaline. In order to add strength in a moment of danger, this hormone spreads a scent that is easily picked up by dogs. A person who sees a dog running after him doesn't know that the animal is actually running to adrenaline's appetizing scent. Of course that scent that retreats while the person runs leads the dog to follow. The scenario written in the mind becomes real. They say, 'You should not run when you see a dog. But if you don't, the animal will attack you.'"

Servant continued:

"What we experienced on the night of the Rescue Operation was no different. Remember what you were actually afraid of when you were walking in the cemetery! Didn't you imagine that the dead there slowly got up from their graves; that slowly dragging their feet, they chased you; and that twenty or thirty of them jumped on you and began biting you?"

Saying, "Exactly," Yağmur was astounded.

"Well, have you lived something like this before that made you imagine these?"

"No, but this is a common scene in the movies I have watched."

"Then you were frightened because you imagined something that had not or would not happen. This means that if you imagine better things in your mind, there will be nothing to fear. To the contrary, everything will be much better..."

"May God be pleased with you! Now I am feeling much better," Yağmur said.

Time for the Evening Prayer had arrived. Servant wanted to add one more thing:

"But I have to warn you on this subject. The days to follow will be more difficult for you. With yesterday's behavior, you showed your seriousness on the subject of being a Servant. They will inform Azazel of this for certain. I want you to memorize this prayer and repeat it every morning after the Morning Prayer:

> *'O my Lord! You have subjected us to an enemy who knows our shame and who sees us although we cannot see him or his tribe. O my Lord! Just as you have made that devil hopeless regarding Your mercy and bereft of Your forgiveness, make him hopeless regarding us as well. Just as You have put distance between him and Your mercy, put distance between us and him as well. For certain You have power over everything.'*

Muhammad ibn Wasi made this prayer every day. While going to the mosque one day, a devil appeared to him and said:

'Hey son of Wasi! Do you recognize me?'

'No, who are you?'

'I am the devil.'

'What do you want from me?'

'The only thing I want is for you not to teach anyone the prayer you recite every morning. In exchange I'll leave you alone.'

In response Muhammad ibn Wasi said:

'I swear by God that I will teach this prayer to whoever wants to learn it. You do your worst!'"

Saying, "From now on be much more careful," Servant had a sweet concern in his voice.

## Day 33

While difficulties became a little more bearable every day, the indescribable joy of drawing closer to his target made Yağmur even more enthusiastic. After performing the Night Prayer with such a joy, he went to sleep with enthusiasm to get up two hours later for the Supererogatory Night Prayer.

No longer needing a clock for waking up, Yağmur woke up exactly two hours later. However, the candle had gone out and there was total darkness. It seemed as if Yağmur had seen a dark entity enter from the mouth of the cave. He immediately recited the prayer he had learned from Servant two days earlier: *A'udhu bi kalimatillahittammati min sharri ma khalaq*. In other words, "I take full refuge in God's words from all the evil of creatures." Then he felt around and found the bag containing his things and took out a new candle and lighter. Just as he was about to light the candle, someone or something from the darkness blew out the candle. When this was repeated several times, he called out to the indistinguishable shadow:

"Who's there?"

Actually he asked this question to be sure of the answer he precipitated. Because the breath that blew out the candle had a smell he recognized well. He had perceived the same smell in Azazel's headquarters. For this reason, the answer did not surprise Yağmur at all:

"I am the one of those who have no one, the friend of the lonely and the goal of those who search."

When Yağmur responded, "Can God's enemy be a friend, vile one? Let me light this candle and then say what you want to say," the following dialogue took place:

"Look at me, young man! Have you become a saint by staying in a cave a couple of days? Don't pretend you are a wise guy or I'll burn you badly."

"If you were really able to do this, you wouldn't hesitate a moment. But you cannot do anything without God's permission."

"And how do you know God hasn't given permission for this?"

"If the one God gives permission and wants to test me, I only ask for patience from Him."

Affected by the fearlessness of the prey before him, the devil deviated to another path:

"Anyway, let's forget about that. Tell me what you're doing here."

"I am teaching Sir Ego, who tried to rebel against me because he is foolish enough to think you are his friend and who was deceived by your promises, that the throne is not vacant."

"What a vain effort. Poor you! When has Sir Ego ever lost hope in me? Someone has fooled you immensely. After all this hunger, thirst, sleeplessness and weariness, what is your gain? Let me tell you: Nothing! When you go outside, again Sir Ego will do whatever I command. He will trick you with Commander Lust and Commander Anger; if not them, then his friends Sleep and Comfort; if not them, then pride, envy, pretense, back-biting or fornication—in short, he will fool you some way. Do you want to be saved from me? Either you surrender to me or you take your life. I even deceived your ancestor Adam; don't you think I can fool you?"

"OK, how about Abraham, Ishmael and Hagar? Why didn't you fool them?"

"Who said I didn't fool them? I fooled them so much...."

"Shut up, vile creature! I saw everything with my own eyes."

"That's true. You are the Servant at the headquarters. My dear, why are you looking at them? They are a Prophet and his family. Anyway, whoever knew what Abraham knew about the Army of Evil would not be fooled by our tricks."

"Don't worry, you dirty liar! I met Dasim, Zalambar, Kamir, Miswat, Sabar, Khumar, Hinzap, Walhan and that vile Awar individually. I will also meet whichever divisions remain. They will meet me too. I am going to cause you a lot of trouble. Actually you should be afraid of me. I am learning one-by-one all of your tricks, games, weapons and weaknesses. Shortly my training will finish and I am going to stand against all of you. I will dedicate my life, spirit, even my eternal bliss in Paradise, if necessary, to save from your clutches those poor people who are uninformed about your tricks, helpless before your games, and without will power when they see your promises!"

Azazel never expected this much. It was obvious that again due to the ineptness of the intelligence gathering division, he had not properly evaluated this man standing before him. With his ingenuity he immediately made a maneuver. He knew from his previous experience that what he was going to say would finish off this conceited man. It was his greatest weapon and he fully trusted it. He took aim and prepared to shoot his last arrow:

"Bravo, young man! I truly congratulate you. Your courage, faith, dedication and determination are commendable. I was very impressed. If an atom of your faith were in someone else's heart, I would lose hope in him. Since the Holy Sphere has groomed you in a special way, it is obvious that you are an exceptional person. In fact, you are so exceptional that from now on even I will be your friend, not your enemy. Anyone who knows what you did and what you believe in would open his heart to you. You can be sure that no harm will come to you from me. I don't want to set out and be bad to someone like you. There was an Umar; when I saw him I changed my path. And now there is you."

He appeared so sincere when he was saying these things that it was obvious why this weapon was so effective. One of his words among all the others had gotten Yağmur's attention. It's a good thing that it did, otherwise, the target would have been hit:

"So after this I am supposed to know you as a friend and not an enemy, huh? After you were thrown out of God's presence and Adam and Eve were being put into Paradise, our Lord made a very important warning. It still echoes in my mind: 'Hey Adam, this devil is certainly the enemy of you and your wife.' Later on I heard another verse from Servant; it explains very well why we have to become a member of the Army of Good and struggle against you: 'For certain the devil is your clear enemy. In that case, you show him enmity as well.' In spite of these you stand up and say, 'Know me as your friend.' You have no friend but yourself. Even those you take to Hell with you will become your enemies there. What friendship are you talking about, O the one who was excluded from God's Mercy forever?"

Azazel was astonished by what had happened. He realized that he shouldn't have said "friendship," but it was too late. He got up and left without saying a word. Neither threat nor diatribe nor praise had been of any help. He didn't neglect to take with him the hope he tied to revenge in order to lighten the pain of his defeat. Of course, this would not be his last encounter with Yağmur.

## Day 40

He had fallen asleep again in order to get up for the Supererogatory Night Prayer. He had become so abstracted from time that if it had not been for those magnificent things he saw in his dream that he was not supposed to describe to anyone until the time came, he would not even have been able to understand that this penitence had ended. Yes, forty days had finished. In the morning he would rise together with the sun. This cave which he had initially seen as a grave had now become a mother's womb for him.

While he was preparing for the Morning Prayer, Servant entered the cave with a smiling face. Saying, "Good tidings to you, Yağmur! You have been accepted with your first penitence. May God increase your faith, service and efforts," he embraced his student.

After the Morning Prayer in which Yağmur acted as imam, they sat down knee-to-knee. There was a new ring in Servant's hand. While taking off the old ring from Yağmur's finger, he said:

"Now I want you to repeat what I say."

He continued:

"My Lord! I am a candidate for servanthood which is a manifestation of Your mercy on Your servant. I swear that

I will fearlessly oppose and, if necessary, give my life in the struggle against Azazel and his followers, the Army of Evil, who are established on Your servants' paths to You, who show goodness to them as difficult, who embellish ugliness, and who have dedicated their lives to this path of rebellion to prevent people from serving You. I promise I will not abandon this struggle for any reason; I will work for 'good' at least as much as they work for 'evil;' I will persevere on this path opened by the Prophets until I attain my goal. I wish for Your help, power, blessings and grace at my side. From the moment I put on this ring which signifies servanthood to You, I will never turn back; I swear this by You, Your Prophets, books and angels. God's light will certainly be completed even if oppressors do not want it to be. Accept this from me, my Lord! Amen!"

This was the same as the ring on Adil's finger. Now he could see the sign on it more clearly. Just as he had guessed, it was a "No u-turn" sign. The only difference was that the line above the "u" turn resembled a "v." Servant carefully placed the ring on Yağmur's finger. Then he looked out of the cave and said:

"We have to hurry. We're late."

"Where to?" Yağmur curiously asked.

"Our plane is at 11.00. We have to hurry in order to stop by at the house."

"OK, but where are we going?"

"I am going to introduce you to such a person that when you see him, your faith in God's mercy will increase. You will say, 'Since God created such a person, then I have no desire except for mercy!' Hurry, Adil is waiting for us below."

# Person of Service

After Yağmur washed up and changed his clothes, they immediately set out. Throughout this journey Servant tried to give information regarding the place they were going. But Yağmur's questions were endless:

"What is the name of this great person?"

"Everyone knows him by a different name. Some say 'Hodja Effendi,' some only say 'My Hodja,' some say 'Sir,' some say 'My Sheik,' and others say 'My Master.' But they are not aware that they are all talking about the same person."

"But how is that possible?"

"Because he appears differently to all of them. Some see him with a long beard, a turban on his head and a wearing a robe; some only see his mustache and well-pressed suit; some see him in an Afghan cap and Afghan dress."

"I still cannot understand this part. I'm sorry."

"Wait, I'll explain it in a way you can understand. People's perceptions are never objective. They always look with certain expectations and they watch to see what they want to see. In other words, there is already an image formed in their minds. When they place what they see on top of the image in their mind, then people appear who look at the same thing, but see different things. Consequently, they like what they see more. This is a mercy for them from God."

"OK, in what shape are we going to see him?"

"It's certain that we both will not see him in the same shape! This is just like looking at the same cloud and seeing different shapes. Actually it's not very surprising."

"But in reality, isn't he just one of these?"

"It is not that easy to know his essence. But if it will relieve your mind, think of it like this. In one era they called him Abu Bakr, later Umar, Uthman and Ali. In later times they called him Shah an-Naqshband, Abdulqadr al-Jilani, Sheik Ahmad Badawi and Ahmad Rufai. At a later time they called him Yunus Emre, Mawlana Rumi, Imam al-Ghazali, Hodja Ahmad Yasawi, and Haji Bayram Wali. In recent times they called him Bediüzzaman Said Nursi, Süleyman Hilmi Tunahan, Abdülhakim Hüseyni, Mahmut Sami Ramazanoğlu, Mehmet Zahit Kotku, Abdülhakim Arvasi and Sultan Baba. In other words, even if the name and body changes, he was actually the same: He was a 'Person of Service' or Servant. He appeared differently and was known differently, but he always did the same work: he served for the salvation of the community of Muhammad and, consequently, for the salvation of all mankind."

"OK, why does a person strive for the salvation of someone else? Does he have to?"

"Let me give you a simple example: Think of an elevator repairman. In order to repair the elevator, he has pulled it up to the top floor and is working on it from the space where he entered from the roof. Realizing later that a tool he needs was left in his car, he leaves the repair work in the middle and goes down. At that moment a person who had gotten on the elevator at the top floor pushes the ground floor button and you can guess what happens. Now do you think that the repairman has any responsibility for this?"

"Of course! He could have at least hung a sign up."

"In fact, let's say that the manager who knows the elevator is being repaired sees that his neighbor has entered the elevator but doesn't say anything. What do you say to this?"

"He's guilty too. He should have at least warned him verbally."

"If you realize it, you said that the repairman should give a written warning and the manager a verbal warning. This is just what we're talking about. There is a written warning about what people should or shouldn't do in regard to behavior that will take them to disaster, and we call it the Qur'an. In addition, there is a special group that warns them verbally when they show this behavior, and we call them Prophets. OK, should a person be quiet because he is not a Prophet? Of course not! Abu Bakr was the first of these. When he thought about people feeling pain, the mercy he felt for them greatly distressed him and he always made this prayer: 'My Lord, please! If necessary, throw me into Hell and increase my body so much that no one else will fit there. Don't let anyone burn but me.'"

With tears in his eyes, Servant continued:

"No one can be expected to have this much mercy, but at least what would you do if you saw someone behaving in a way that would lead them to Hell? We call the answer to this question 'Service.' Because otherwise you will be held responsible in the next life for not warning people just like the repairman or the manager."

"You're right! It is not possible to keep quiet when people do something they will regret later on and for which they will say, 'If only we had not done that; if only someone had warned us,' and to say, 'You'll see what happens.'"

"Let's say that while your mother, whom you call 'Valide Sultan' because you love and respect her so much, is walking on a street, a purse-snatcher struggles with her and tries to take the handbag on her arm. At that moment, not able to endure the fear, her heart stops."

"God forbid!"

"Of course, God forbid. In fact, in order to protect her, God has one of His servants there ready to protect her. But in spite of the fact that this man saw what was happening and had the strength to stop the purse-snatcher, he didn't do anything. Now, wouldn't you be angry with this man and make a claim against him in the next life?"

"I understand very well what you mean to say."

"Yağmur, if someone doesn't spread good among people and stand up against every kind of evil, think of what kind of state society would be in. Consequently, since we were sent to this world as the vice-gerents of God, then you can imagine that just as it is our duty to perform all services necessary on His behalf, what great treachery it would be to turn our backs on these duties."

"Absolutely! You expressed it very well when we first met. You said, 'Which of us is not Servant?' It is very true that in every case we will pass our lives in the service of someone. I have chosen to serve God. I have begun to see that my purpose of existing is to serve His servants in order to gain His acceptance. *Inshallah* (God willing), my Lord will not turn me back from this path."

While saying these things, Yağmur was also looking at his ring which was a sign of all these words.

As soon as they got off the plane, they performed their Prayers. A person waiting for them in the mosque came up to them after the Prayers and said:

"I have come to take you, gentlemen. Please come with me."

...

Every kilometer of this long trip on land increased Yağmur's excitement a little more. According to what Servant said, he would see in this world how God manifested his mercy in one body. His excitement was at a peak when the car stopped in front of a lovely private house in a garden.

The young man who had brought them here immediately ran and opened the door and invited them inside. Orderly in every aspect and very plain, this house's interi-

or gave peace to a person. Saying, "Follow me," Servant turned towards the stairway, and Yağmur followed. Passing several doors lined up on the upstairs floor, they came to a two-winged door at the end of the corridor. Almost hearing his heartbeats with his ears, Yağmur took a deep breath before he entered the door. When Servant knocked on the door and went in, he followed head-down.

What he saw when he raised his head amazed him... Because there was no one there. When Servant said: "Come here and sit down and let's wait," Yağmur was a little relieved thinking that this was not extraordinary. He sat down exactly where Servant had told him to sit.

There was not a sound in the room. The expected person's being able to enter the room at any moment had turned Yağmur into stone. Of course, with him like that, there was a general silence—until Servant broke it:

"I'll leave you both alone."

"I didn't understand. What did you say?"

"I said that I'll go out and leave the two of you alone."

Quickly looking around, Yağmur understood only one thing from all this uncertainty: There was no end to Servant's surprises.

# The Stranger in the Mirror

"Excuse me, but I don't see anyone but you in the room," Yağmur said.

"Look straight across from yourself; what do you see?" Servant asked.

"A mirror."

"OK, then what do you see in the mirror?"

"Myself."

"Yes! As I told you: When you look, isn't it the best person where the manifestation of God's mercy can be seen? Regardless of who you hoped to see here, wasn't his worth only going to be as much as the value you give him? Two Umars were looking at the same person; one said 'Prophet' and the other said 'Sorcerer.' In other words, the matter begins and ends with you, Yağmur. Look carefully at the mirror. It is not an ordinary mirror. There is an important reason you have made this journey. But don't ever forget this! Put this process aside in your mind and have faith in what you will soon see."

Having said these words, Servant left the room.

Yağmur stood up and approached the mirror. He pulled over a chair and sat down just in front of the mirror. He couldn't see anything but himself.

There was one Yağmur sitting on the chair. On the one hand, he was trying to put aside his mind. When he was able to do this, he surrendered to what would happen. At that time the image in the mirror began to move. Just as it was sitting motionless on the chair a little earlier like Yağmur, now it began to speak:

"Finally we have been able to meet."

Now he understood much better why he had to put his mind aside. Because what he saw was not something the mind could grasp. The Yağmur in the mirror continued talking:

"For years you numbed me with the television you watched and the food you ate that was mixed with forbidden things and you forgot me. I was nothing more than a prisoner of the Army of Evil for all this time. Thank God, you finally rescued me from captivity."

"OK, but who are you?"

"I am you. When someone mentions you, I am the person they mean. I am the addressee of God's commands and prohibitions. I am the Yağmur who has been held for years in the prison in the Cave of Heedlessness. However, with your efforts and the help of elders I am finally free. Just as you rescued your throne from the hands of Azazel, now it is time to rescue others."

"The help of which elders are you talking about?"

"The Servants before me, of course. Who do you think helped us in the battle we fought with the Army of Evil in the Valley of Faith? That was a sacred army commanded by Abraham and comprised of Servants. For you have heard that they are not to be called dead. They are alive in God's presence. A little later I am going to show all of them to you one by one. Think of this mirror as the mirror of your heart. Just as you are talking with me now, you will also be able to consult with them like this. However, this will take some time. When you succeed in always keeping your heart mirror clean and make it shine with remembrance of God, those elders will begin to appear here one by one. You will see them in this form for a certain time. In exchange for not watching television, you can watch them in the mirrors. At the next stage when you close your eyes, they will appear in the mirror of your heart. In order for you to recognize them when they appear, I am going to introduce you to all of them with their names."

The image in the mirror began to change.

The images of however many Servants had been named by Servant before began to appear in the mirror. After one was introduced by name, the next appeared. Yağmur engraved hundreds in his memory like this. At the end his image again appeared and completed its words like this:

"Go now Yağmur! Just as Servant rescued me from captivity, you save people from the captivity of the Army of Evil, from the captivity of its most powerful weapon, television, from the captivity of forbidden things, from the captivity of heedlessness and laziness together with all sins.

Go Yağmur! Go so that thrones do not remain vacant and hearts do not remain without rain!"

Then the image disappeared... or Yağmur could not see it because of his tears. After he came to himself a little, he left the room and went downstairs. The man who had brought them from the airport said that Servant was in the back yard and he pointed to the door opening to the garden.

There was beauty here that could not have been anticipated from the front of the house. A magnificent "Plane Tree" in the middle of the garden which was adorned with many flowers, some of which he had seen before and some not, caught Yağmur's attention. As for Servant, he was peacefully sitting leaned against this huge tree with the same smile on his face. His eyes were closed, he had prayer beads in his hand, and who knows what kind of dhikr was on his tongue.

A little later he opened his eyes and said to Yağmur who was busy with the flowers:

"Let's go! Our friends and enemies are waiting for us."

They set out on the road to the airport. Yağmur still didn't know where they were. He was looking around carefully and looking for a clue, but still he couldn't understand. In the end he found asking to be the solution, but he tried not to do it at least for once and he decided not to. Asking about even the smallest things he felt curiosity about in his life, Yağmur now refrained from asking such an important thing, hoping to show his surrender to Servant. Actually aware of this, Servant was happy on behalf of this intelligent student who learned many things in a short period of time.

Not speaking more than two sentences since they came, the driver said, "Have a good trip," and they boarded the plane.

Approximately ten minutes after they took off, Servant took an envelope out of his pocket and gave it to Yağmur.

"This envelope was sent for you. Welcome among us," he said.

Yağmur took out the paper from the envelope and carefully read it:

"From: The Army of Good, Messengers' Unit, Intelligence Headquarters

To: Servant Yağmur

First I would like to congratulate you for being honored with a sacred duty like servanthood and inform you that you have been assigned as a member of the Alliance of the Virtuous due to your special capabilities. You will be informed of the duties and authority of this 'Special Operations Team' at the first opportunity.

In regard to your first assignment:

Don't allow anything strange that you will notice from the moment you return to your home bother you. This is not just an attack on your family, but a world-wide operation begun by the Army of Evil. As a Servant, it is your duty to save all innocent people—first of all your wife—who have been subjected to this attack.

Details and necessary material will be sent to you later.

I wish you success in this difficult duty and ask for assistance from God and the angels.

Messengers' Unit

Chief of Intelligence"

Yağmur put the paper back into the envelope and looked into Servant's eyes, seeking some consolation. At that moment he saw so much pain in those eyes that his own pain became nothing in comparison. Holding Yağmur's hand, Servant said the most beautiful thing that could be said at that moment:

*If suffering comes from Divine Majesty,*
*Or fidelity from Divine Beauty,*
*Both are a delight to the soul,*
*Pleasing in Your blessings, pleasing in Your wrath.*

To be continued in *The Black Box Operation...*